ROAD RAGE

From the corner of my eye I saw the driver of the blue Ford pick up speed. He put on his turn signal, then pulled out in front of me. As he drew even with me, he threw up his index finger like he was pulling the trigger of a gun. The Ford slowed, then shot past me along the deserted road. . . .

When I noticed the blue Ford again, it was ahead of me, the driver moving less than twenty miles per hour. I slowed. As I did, he put on his signal to pull off to the side of the road, as if he had a flat tire. I drove past, looking for any sign of car distress. There was none. But as I pulled past, I noticed the baby's car seat strapped behind him.

The whole encounter took less than a minute and I wouldn't have thought any more about it except the Ford soon caught up with me again. This time the driver didn't pass. He was driving so close behind me that I thought he was going to ram my tail end. I glanced at the rearview mirror. The driver was staring at me unblinkingly. Something in the look on his face told me that this man would hurt me if he ever got the chance. . . .

D1007532

Bantam Books by Nora DeLoach

Mama Stalks the Past
Mama Rocks the Empty Cradle

and coming soon
from Bantam Books

Mama Pursues Murderous Shadows

Mama rocks the empty cradle

NORA DeLOACH

BANTAM BOOKS
NEW YORK
TORONTO
LONDON
SYDNEY
AUCKLAND

This edition contains the complete text
of the original hardcover edition.
NOT ONE WORD HAS BEEN OMITTED.

MAMA ROCKS THE EMPTY CRADLE
A Bantam Book

PUBLISHING HISTORY
Bantam hardcover edition / 1998
Bantam mass market edition / November 1999

All rights reserved.
Copyright © 1998 by Nora DeLoach
Cover art copyright © 1999 by David F. Henderson

No part of this book may be reproduced or transmitted
in any form or by any means, electronic or mechanical,
including photocopying, recording, or by any information
storage and retrieval system, without permission
in writing from the publisher.
For information address: Bantam Books

If you purchased this book without a cover you should be
aware that this book is stolen property. It was reported
as "unsold or destroyed" to the publisher and neither
the author nor the publisher has received any payment
for this "stripped book."

ISBN 0-553-57720-4

Published simultaneously in the United States and Canada

Bantam Books are published by Bantam Books, a division of
Random House, Inc. Its trademark, consisting of the words
"Bantam Books" and the portrayal of a rooster, is Registered
in U.S. Patent and Trademark Office and in other countries.
Marca Registrada. Bantam Books, 1540 Broadway,
New York, New York 10036.

PRINTED IN THE UNITED STATES OF AMERICA

OPM   10 9 8 7 6 5 4 3 2 1

Dedication

To *William, Sr.*, my husband of thirty-four years; *Edwin*, my oldest son; *Shekinah*, my daughter (and best friend); *Vincent*, my son-in-law; their sons, *Joshua*, my first grandchild, and *Cedric*, the newest addition to our family; *William, Jr.*, my youngest son; *Stacey*, his wife; *Delcena*, my niece; *Richard*, her husband; and *Morgan*, their daughter.

Mama rocks the empty cradle

ONE

The midday heat was desertlike. Soybean husks seasoned the air. Midnight stopped to sniff a clump of kudzu, then crossed a makeshift bridge which led to an almost hidden path. He was near the large branch that made a shadowy tunnel overhead. He sniffed again. The air smelled of rain.

The dog's coat gleamed ebony. He walked forward slowly, wagging his tail, then stopped to bark at a squirrel who, after scampering up a tree, turned and stared contemptuously down into his eyes. The sounds of singing birds filled the darkening July sky. The Labrador lumbered toward the carpet of leaves. It had been a little over six months since he last stood under the huge oak that flanked the old house.

The shack's door squeaked in the rising wind.

Midnight eyed the red-tipped shrubbery, then began digging. Overhead, what started as a gentle sprinkle quickly turned into a downpour. Midnight headed home.

It was dark and wet when the dog walked into his backyard. He barked. The door opened. Midnight smelled food; love and warmth were inside. A tall dark man patted his head. "What you got there, boy?" he asked.

Midnight's tail wagged as he dropped the infant's skull at his master's feet.

CHAPTER
ONE

I'd failed.

Frustration hung over my head like a halo. The task hadn't been hard. My boss had given me a routine assignment, one that normally took me less than a week to do. "Run a paper trail, find this witness; our client swears he exists," he'd said. Then he gave me a name, a description, and an approximate age.

When I didn't come up with the person, my boss, one of Atlanta's best defense lawyers, plea-bargained for his client. Then he boarded a plane from Hartsfield to take a European vacation.

I sat, staring at a diploma that I'd taken so much pride in earning, and thinking about the day I'd interviewed for the position of paralegal in Sidney Jacoby's research department. I'd already had five such interviews in less prestigious law offices without a hint of a job offer.

Except for my urge to flick dandruff from his shoulders, I swiftly sized Sidney Jacoby up to be pretty cool. Sidney looked down at my résumé, then back up to meet my eyes. "Simone Covington," he said, as if he liked the sound of my name.

I nodded.

"Graduated from Emory, I see."

"Yes," I said.

"Are you going on to law school?"

"No," I admitted. "I like the legal research."

Sidney laughed. "I like the research myself," he admitted. "Did a lot of that when I was in law school."

"You were a paralegal?" I asked, surprised.

"Yes," he said, shaking his head, his dark brown eyes twinkling in a way that made me sure he could be warm with compassion at one moment and cold at the next. He leaned back in his seat, and crossed his fingers in front of him. "Nobody can tamper with the truth," he continued. "If you dig deep enough, peel off all the layers of appearances, cut away through the lies, and strip through the absurdities, you'll find the truth, Miss Covington."

I smiled.

"The adrenaline you feel from the experience is priceless," he said.

My eyes widened. I believed the man, believed he shared my passion for getting to the heart of things.

"When I was a boy," he continued, "I almost

drove my mother crazy. Later, after I'd finished law school, my father died. I offered to move back home, thinking I could help her. She wouldn't have it. She even gave me five thousand dollars and told me, 'I cannot take another day of your questioning everything and everybody that comes to my house.' "

We laughed.

"My teachers loved me," I said. "They could always count on me to research the things that they couldn't find time to research themselves."

Sidney said, "I could never do anything that other kids called fun, but I knew the details of just about anything. And the things I didn't know, I wouldn't stop until I learned them."

"I suppose we have a gift," I heard myself say.

"Yes," he agreed, as if I had said something profound. His eyes twinkled. "And don't you ever take that gift for granted, Simone Covington."

The next day, Sidney Jacoby telephoned me and made me a generous offer. Needless to say, I like the man. To be honest, from that day forward, I felt good about working for him. He genuinely believed in what I do, and he supported the way I do it.

I've worked for Sidney for five years now, five years in which he had never taken a vacation. Oh, he'd planned to get away, all right—every detail of a six-week tour of Europe from the time the plane leaves Hartsfield until it lands in London, he had planned. But he had never done it.

When I admitted that I'd come up empty-handed in my search for our witness, Sidney didn't say much. But I was sure he was disappointed. I suppose that's why I was thinking about the day he had interviewed me, remembering our mutual belief in digging until we got what we sought.

Still studying my diploma, I reached for a box of Godiva chocolates and my phone and called my mama. "Sidney's gone on vacation," I told her.

"Good, then you can take some time off, too—come home," she replied.

"Just because Sidney is out of town doesn't mean that there isn't any work for me to do."

"It's midsummer. Sidney needed a vacation and you do, too."

"When I told Sidney that I couldn't come up with his witness," I told Mama, "he stared like he saw something in me that he'd missed all these years—"

"Simone," Mama interrupted. "You're doing it again. Overreacting. It's normal for people to take vacations in the summer and Sidney is normal. Besides, if that witness existed, you *would* have found him. Sidney and I both know that!"

I swallowed. "Maybe that's why he didn't push me to keep looking," I said, my spirit lightening.

Mama's voice was softer. "Forget the case. Take a week's vacation and come home—I need you."

"You want help to solve another murder?" I asked, and laughed.

Mama laughed too, a light, musical sound. "Not this time," she told me. "I'm scheduled for surgery first thing Monday morning."

I sat up straight. "What kind of surgery?" I demanded. "What's wrong with you?"

"Nothing serious," Mama replied. "I'm just having bunions removed from both my feet. I'd planned for James to go with me to the hospital—"

"Hospital?"

"It's outpatient surgery, Simone," Mama said. "Anyway, you'd be a big help to me. With Sidney out of the country for six weeks, you can spare a week of your vacation, can't you?"

"Cliff—" I started to say.

"You and Cliff will have at least two weeks left to do something together. But, tell you what I'll do," Mama said, and I knew I was about to be bribed. "You come home on Friday, you and I will shop and cook on Saturday, then Cliff can drive here and have Sunday dinner with you, me, and your father."

My boyfriend, Cliff, is a divorce lawyer who is working hard to become a partner in his firm. The thought of how much Cliff and I both loved Mama's cooking whirled through my mind. "Cliff has been pretty busy with another one of his detachment clients," I said.

"Divorces seem to be plentiful these days," Mama commented.

I nodded although she couldn't see me. "It's worst when a client thinks her divorce lawyer should be at her disposal every minute of the day."

Mama didn't say anything.

"How long will you need me?" I asked again. My

spirit rose at the thought of eating another one of my mama's meals.

"A week," she said.

"A week," I repeated, thinking that Sidney would surely expect me to use *some* of my vacation time while he was gone, especially to take care of my mama.

My mama's name is Grace, but she's called Candi because of her candied sweet potato complexion.

My parents are originally from Otis, South Carolina. They got married right out of high school and my father joined the Air Force. After a career of thirty years and the birth of my two brothers (Rodney and Will) and me, Captain James Covington retired and he and Mama moved back home to Otis, a town of five thousand people.

"Okay," I told Mama, "but I want you to cook roast pork, fried chicken, collard greens, macaroni and cheese, string beans and new potatoes, rice and okra. And, for dessert, I want carrot cake and sweet potato pie."

On Saturday morning, we were in Winn Dixie shopping for groceries when the baby's wail rang through the aisles. It sounded like somebody had stuck a hand down the infant's throat and squeezed its intestines.

I flinched. Mama held her shopping list in one hand, a can of mushroom soup in the other. She was saying something about sodium when the child's second scream broke her concentration. She glanced in the direction of the cry. "Something is wrong with that child!" she said softly, putting the can of soup back on the shelf.

A voice over the loudspeaker suggested that shoppers visit the produce section . . . watermelon, grapes, and peaches were on sale. Then one of my favorite songs by the Manhattans began to be piped through the store.

Mama eased her shopping cart toward the juices; I hummed along with the music.

The baby screamed again, the sound as sharp as a police siren. Mama looked at me; I threw her a look of reluctance, but it didn't do any good. She was going to see what the matter was with that child and that was all there was to it. I shrugged, then followed her toward the noise.

On the next aisle, near the canned vegetables, we spotted a woman who looked all of thirty-five years old, who smelled powerfully like the camphor used for canker sores. She was holding a baby and shaking it. The woman's skin was dark. She had small eyes, and a very large nose. As we walked toward her, she looked scared, almost terrified.

I glanced at the baby . . . it was beautiful, although

its tiny face was as red as the labels on the cans of tomatoes that were on the shelf. It wailed again.

"Birdie Smiley, what's wrong with that baby?" Mama demanded.

Birdie stammered but she didn't stop shaking the baby in her arms. "I—I had no business—"

Mama interrupted impatiently, "That's Cricket's baby, Morgan. What have you done to that child?"

Birdie didn't look up. Instead, she began shaking the baby harder. The baby screamed.

"Stop that!" Mama shouted, then she snatched the crying baby from Birdie's arms. "If you keep that up you'll knock the wind out of her—she'll stop breathing!"

Birdie's body was trembling. Beads of sweat were on her forehead. "I—I ain't got no business keeping her . . . ain't got no business letting her come with me . . . I just remembered, I ain't got no business keeping nobody's baby!" The words poured from her mouth like a hot flood.

Mama was cradling the sobbing baby in her arms, looking down into its wide-open eyes. "Now, Morgan," she whispered. "Everything is going to be all right!"

"I ain't got no business keeping a baby," Birdie stammered. "Doctor told me I ain't got the nerves for it . . . ain't got no business . . . can't take care of no baby . . . won't do it again!"

The baby hiccuped and stopped crying. "I was at the hospital the day this baby was born," Mama said, as if talking to herself. "She had the brightest eyes, and when you talked to her, she paid attention like she understood exactly what you were saying."

I looked closer at Morgan. She was indeed enchanting. For a moment, I felt a strange inkling, like the prickle of an unfamiliar emotion. Morgan's eyes charmed me, too.

"Is Birdie some kin to Morgan?" I asked, thinking that such a nervous woman had no business taking care of this delightful baby.

"I don't think she is," Mama answered. "Cricket Childs, Morgan's mother, is one of my clients." Mama works for the Social Services Department.

"Then this beautiful child is the other side of the coin of a single-parent home," I said.

"I suppose," Mama replied, in a tone that told me that she didn't think my statement relevant.

As long as Morgan held on to my eyes, I had to agree with Mama. This captivating baby girl looked almost a year old. She had thick black hair and a flawless milk-chocolate complexion. Her eyes were dark and bright, her mouth small and round. She smelled of Johnson's baby powder. But cuteness wasn't all there was to this little girl. There was something bewitching about that child's gaze.

Mama smiled down at Morgan, clearly having fallen in love. This baby's bright beckoning eyes had that kind of power. "I can't imagine Cricket leaving you, sweet child," Mama whispered.

Birdie Smiley stood anxiously rubbing her arm and staring at Mama and little Morgan when Sarah Jenkins, Annie Mae Gregory, and Carrie Smalls eased up quietly beside Mama. In Otis, these three women are jokingly called the "town historians" because they go out of their way to know everything about everybody in Otis. Mama actually finds them helpful. She calls them her "source."

I was surprised to see the ladies, but Mama glanced at them as if she'd known all along that they were in the store. "Ladies," she said, without taking her attention from the smiling baby, "it's good to see you."

"I told you," Sarah Jenkins said, her voice strong despite her pasty complexion and constant preoccupation with her health, "that was Cricket's baby hollering."

Annie Mae Gregory is an obese woman, whose body is the shape of a perfect oval and who has dark circles around her stonelike eyes; Annie Mae always reminds me of a big fat raccoon. When she looks at you a certain way, she appears cross-eyed. She asked Mama, her jaws shaking like Jell-O, "Candi, what are you doing with Cricket Childs's baby?"

"I ain't got no business—" Birdie Smiley muttered, as if talking to herself again.

Mama glanced up. "Now, Birdie, Morgan is just fine now."

Carrie Smalls is a tall woman with a small mouth and a sharp nose. She holds her body straight, like she's practiced so that her shoulders wouldn't slump—I've told Mama more than once that it's Carrie Smalls who gives strength to the three women's presence, who gives a measure of credibility to what these three say. Carrie Smalls looks the youngest; she dyes her hair jet black and lets it hang to her shoulders. Now she looked down into Mama's arms at the baby girl. "Where's Cricket?" she asked, in an authoritarian tone.

Just about that time, Koot Rawlins, a large woman known for being full of gas, swung into the aisle and belched. Koot's shopping cart was full of lima beans, rice, fatback bacon, and Pepsi. She nodded a greeting but kept walking.

I went back to staring down into little Morgan's face. "My friend Yasmine, the beautician, she had a party a few weeks ago—a young woman named Cricket was there who told me she lived in Otis. Could she be this baby's mother?" I asked.

Mama's attention shifted back between me and the baby as if she was surprised. "There's only one Cricket Childs that lives in this town, and she's Morgan's mother, yes."

Annie Mae Gregory shook her head impatiently. "Where in the world is Cricket now?" she snapped.

Sarah Jenkins looked around. "I declare, Cricket's got her share of faults—"

"Whatever Cricket's faults," Mama interrupted, "she's a good mother. I can personally vouch for her devotion to this child."

Carrie Smalls shrugged. "I reckon you think 'cause your job throw you to be with her that you know her better than anybody else. My question now is where is Cricket, and why is she letting her baby cause so much confusion in this grocery store?"

"Cricket isn't far," Mama said, convincingly. "She must have left Morgan with Birdie for just a few minutes."

Carrie Smalls motioned to her two companions that it was time for them to leave. "You work for the welfare, Candi," she told my mother. "You know better than anybody else that if Cricket doesn't take better care of her child, it'll be your place to take her away from Cricket and put her in a home where she'd be properly taken care of. A grocery store ain't no place to drop off a child—"

"I don't think it's fair to say that Cricket dropped Morgan off in the store," Mama pointed out. "Birdie is taking care of the baby."

Carrie Smalls responded sharply, "There are times when Birdie can't take care of her own self, much less take care of a hollering baby!"

I watched the three women shuffle down the aisle toward the fruit and vegetables. But Mama ignored them. She was still staring at the baby in her arms. "We'll find your mama, sweetheart," she whispered. Her words seemed to hold the child's attention.

Suddenly, I decided I shouldn't be a part of this scene. Let me explain. I—I . . . well, I just don't have a very strong maternal instinct. Don't get me wrong, that doesn't mean I don't like babies—it's just that they don't turn me on like I'm told they are supposed to do!

My girlfriend Yasmine, the one I told you about who fixes hair, is a voluptuous young woman who had her nose job long before plastic surgery became a part of black folks' thing. Yasmine is about my age, unmarried, no children. And like me, she's in a monogamous relationship. Her friend's name is Ernest and while Yasmine won't admit it, I know she wants Ernest to ask her to marry him so that she could have a house full of babies. Yasmine and I could be walking inside the mall, she'll see a baby and her eyes will light up. She starts with "ain't she cute," or "she's so precious," going on and on until I feel like I am going to gag. If the mother of the baby allows, Yasmine even starts talking gibberish that she swears the baby understands. . . . The whole thing drives me crazy!

I've told Yasmine over and over again that the strong feeling for motherhood that she claims is normal just ain't there for me. "Girlfriend," she says, "something is *seriously* wrong with any black woman that ain't turned on by a baby!"

I have to admit there are times when I find myself wondering whether Yasmine is right. For instance, as Morgan's eyes drew me to her like a bee to honey, I found myself wondering what it would be like to have a daughter, and perhaps to have the kind of relationship with her the same as Mama has with me. That thought scared me. After all, I wasn't Candi Covington. How could I be sure that I could pull off the maternal thing as successfully as she had? Anyway, I didn't want to dwell on that thought, so I decided that seeing Mama hold tiny Morgan to her breast, hearing her speak soft, kind words, and seeing Morgan respond with a bubble of spit and cooing sounds *wasn't* what I needed to be watching right now.

Birdie Smiley, whose bottom lip trembled and who hadn't spoken since Sarah Jenkins, Annie Mae Gregory, and Carrie Smalls had moved on, now stepped backward, knocking down a few cans from the shelf.

Mama didn't look at Birdie. "Morgan," she was saying, "you are a pretty little thing, now aren't you?"

I remembered I wanted some Famous Amos so I turned and walked toward the cookie row. I stopped for a moment to taste the sample of vanilla pudding a demonstrator was handing out. I nodded, thinking of how the pudding would go well with the cookies that I'd already decided I was going to buy and stash in the trunk of my car.

A few minutes later, I was standing in the ten-items-or-less checkout line when I saw Sheriff Abe, his deputy Rick Martin, and Cricket Childs run into the store like they were going to put out a fire. Something was wrong. I decided to forget about paying for the cookies.

In the back of the store, a crowd had formed around Birdie, Mama, Morgan, Sheriff Abe, Deputy Rick Martin, and Cricket. I had to push past Sarah Jenkins, Annie Mae Gregory, and Carrie Smalls just to get next to Mama, who still held Morgan. Snatching the baby from Mama's arms, Cricket was glaring at Birdie Smiley as if she knew it wasn't Mama who meant her baby harm. "You've got a serious problem, crazy woman!" Cricket yelled.

Birdie's slightly crossed eyes had a pitiful look in them.

Cricket tapped her forehead. "You stole my baby from my car in broad daylight!"

Mama's eyes widened. "You didn't ask Birdie to keep your baby?" she asked Cricket.

Cricket's nostrils flared; she held her baby close to her breast. "She stole Morgan from my car when I went into the Shell station to pay for gas! Thank goodness the lady in the store recognized Birdie's station wagon. And thank goodness Miss Blanche drove up and told us that she'd just seen Birdie walk into this store with Morgan in her arms!"

Spasms twisted Birdie's plain face, like she had inner pain.

Sheriff Abe motioned to his deputy to disperse the gathering crowd. "Okay, folks," Rick Martin said, his voice rising above the loudspeaker music, an old Beatles song. "Things are under control now. So go about your business, go on with your shopping."

"*Nobody* is going to leave this store until Cricket and Birdie go!" Carrie Smalls declared loudly.

Deputy Martin walked over and gently took Birdie's arm. "I'm sorry, but you're going to have to come with me," he told her.

"If you touch my baby again, I'll kill you, you hear me?" Cricket shrilled, and in her arms little Morgan whimpered. "You're messing with the wrong black woman."

Birdie bit her bottom lip. Her eyes blinked uncontrollably. But she didn't say a word. Mama studied Birdie's face.

Sheriff Abe, who had known Birdie all her life, spoke. "You come on with me and Rick now," he told Birdie. "We'll get this thing settled properly."

"I'll kill you stiff dead," Cricket said, clutching Morgan so hard the baby started to cry again.

Mama's eyebrows shot up. "Take it easy," she said to Cricket.

"I'll *kill* her if she lays another hand on my baby!"

"No harm has come to Morgan," Mama pointed out. But she looked worried.

"If she so much as looks at my Morgan again, I'll *kill* her. I swear!"

Sheriff Abe eased between Cricket and Birdie.

"Now that you've got that beautiful child back, why don't you take her home?" Mama suggested gently.

Cricket looked down at Morgan and her face lit up. "Don't you *ever* put your hands on my baby again," she warned Birdie Smiley. "If you touch my Morgan again, your behind is mine and nobody is going to keep me from it!"

We watched Cricket sashay away, swearing loud enough for everybody inside and outside of the store to hear her. Abe and Rick waited until she was driving out of the parking lot before they led Birdie toward their patrol car.

"Cricket isn't the most modest girl," Mama said to me, her eyes following Abe and Rick. "Actually, the girl is a bit on the wild side. I've spent more than a few hours trying to get her to tone down, think about her reputation in this town. I can't say she's paid much attention to what I've told her, though. Still, I know that she loves her baby. I'm convinced that she'd die for Morgan, if it ever came to that. No, it doesn't surprise me, the way Cricket acted. But, Birdie— It just ain't her nature to do something like stealing a baby from an automobile."

"Maybe Birdie's crazy," I said, looking down at my Famous Amos cookies and wondering how many calories were in the whole package. "She certainly acted like she was unbalanced."

Mama shook her head sadly. "I admit there must be something seriously wrong with Birdie. There's no other reason I can think of for her to steal that baby in broad daylight and then bring her inside this store where a crowd of people would see them."

By now even the nosiest shoppers were moving on. Mama sighed. "You know, Simone, I've worked with both Birdie and her husband, Isaiah, doing volunteer work at the community center with our young people. I've never seen her so confused."

I shrugged. My mind wandered on to Cliff and the way he smiles like Richard Roundtree; the man drives me crazy. "We need to get home. I'm expecting Cliff to call," I said, changing the subject from Birdie and children.

Mama nodded as if she knew that my interest in

the events that had just taken place had already
waned.

I looked down into our shopping cart. We still
hadn't picked up the pork roast or the chickens.
"Let's get this over with," I told Mama, thinking of
the wonderful meals she had promised me.

CHAPTER
TWO

As she had promised, Mama did her thing. Our Sunday dinner was a deliciously signatured Candi Covington. After we'd eaten, Mama and I cleaned the kitchen. My father and Cliff sat in the family room drinking Heineken while Daddy told Cliff every detail of my childhood.

I'm convinced that, to keep on my father's good side, Cliff acted like he enjoyed these stories. Every time my father stopped talking, Cliff would pop a beer and ask him another question.

By seven o'clock, my father seemed satisfied with Cliff's attentiveness. (Besides that, all of the beer was gone.) Mama suggested that Daddy lie down for a while but, of course, he wouldn't consider that. He said he had to make a trip to his buddy Coal's house. Coal lived in the town of Darien, a fifteen-minute drive from Otis.

Mama went to her room to, as she said, make a few phone calls. (I suspected to call Coal to tell him to keep an eye out for my father, although she'd never admit to it.)

My parents had remodeled the back of their home the past spring. A wall had been torn out and double-hung floor-to-ceiling windows had been installed; the new look gave the kitchen and the adjoining family room the illusion that they were completely glass. Both rooms now opened into a backyard garden of herbaceous borders, fragrant roses, and gardenias. Azaleas thrived under the limbs of a big oak tree, and a new chain-link fence was bordered with bright annuals.

Cliff and I sat outside in the garden. Daddy's dog, Midnight, stretched out at our feet. I'd told Cliff that my visit to Otis would last a week because of Mama's surgery. Cliff had news for me, too. He would be going to L.A. His stay would be a minimum of two weeks. His most vocal client, Mrs. Campbell, wanted him near while she inventoried one of the houses that were being sold as part of her divorce settlement.

We sat and talked and watched the summer sun set over peaceful Otis until nine o'clock, when Cliff headed back to Atlanta.

My parents' bedroom had a freshness to it, like linen that had been washed in bleach and hung outside to dry. Sunlight from a skylight overhead streaked across the floor, illuminating a cherry TV/VCR armoire. It had glass knobs and a bottom pull-down door. Mama loved that armoire—she'd bought it for herself in celebration of obtaining her bachelor's degree from the University of the State of New York Regents External Degree program.

Their bed was a four-poster, cherry, like the armoire. The windows were draped in white Priscilla curtains with tiebacks. On the floor was a Persian rug, something that my father had gotten on the black market during one of his tours near the Persian Gulf.

It was Tuesday morning, nine-thirty A.M. to be exact. Twenty-four hours had passed since Mama had her bunions removed. She lay in the four-poster bed, her feet propped up on a stack of large pillows. The doctor had told me to make sure her feet stayed elevated above her heart. Mama had a concerned expression on her face, like something was on her mind. I surmised it was because she was so helpless, something *very* rare.

I'd cooked her breakfast, nothing as elaborate as she would have fixed for me had it been I who was incapacitated—whole wheat toast, jelly, coffee, and two scrambled eggs. I suspected the eggs were a little runny but I didn't want to overcook them. Mama had chided me more than once for scrambling eggs too hard.

Now she looked down at her plate and smiled. The glint in her eyes told me that she was wondering whether she could live through a week of my cooking. Still, she said in a voice that sounded genuinely grateful, "Thanks, honey." I told her it was no problem and went to call my office.

Minutes after I'd gotten off the telephone after touching base with Sidney's secretary, Shirley, the phone rang. Back in Mama's room, I answered it, thinking that maybe Shirley had forgotten to tell me something.

"Candi?" a familiar voice on the other end asked.

"No," I answered. "This is Simone."

"Is Candi able to talk on the phone?" the voice asked.

"Just a minute," I said, putting the phone down and reaching for Mama's tray. "Sheriff Abe wants to talk to you," I told her.

Mama nodded, then reached over and picked up the receiver. She said hello, but didn't say another word for several minutes. A couple of times she nodded, as if to herself, but for the most part she held the phone to her ear, listening. Finally, she said goodbye, then hung the phone up. When she looked up at me, she shook her head. "Cricket Childs is dead!"

"An accident?" I asked.

There was an extreme sadness in my mother's face. "She was murdered. Clarence Young, who used to run with Cricket about three years ago, found her in his Cherry Ridge apartment. He told Abe that he'd been out of town working for over a week.

When he got back home early this morning, he found Cricket's body sprawled out on his bed. She was stabbed to death."

"How terrible," I gasped. Then I asked, "Where is her baby?"

"I guess Morgan is with one of Cricket's people," Mama answered. "That poor little baby."

For the first time I noticed the sound of rain hitting the bedroom window. It pricked an urging in the bottom of my stomach, a distinct message from my bladder. "I've got to go to the bathroom," I said.

Mama nodded, her eyebrows raised resignedly as she reached for her breakfast tray.

While I was in the bathroom, I thought about the first time I'd met Cricket Childs, at Yasmine's party. She was a tall girl whose head strutted two sets of weave. A cluster of curls on top, just above the crown, looked like a bowl of strawberries. Below the crown and two inches past her shoulders she'd had long straight hair that shone like it had been waxed. Her complexion was mocha and her green dress fit her body like a wet suit. Cricket had a good figure except for her narrow behind that stuck out like a wad of chewing gum. Still, she was very pretty.

I'd seen Yasmine hand her a drink and the next time I noticed Cricket, she must have had a few whiskey sours in her because her voice rose above the crowd and four foul words spilled from her mouth like a torrent.

The rest of the evening I either saw Cricket rubbing her behind up against any male she could get next to or telling raunchy jokes that she ended up admitting were personal experiences. When Cricket seemed to target Cliff as her rubbing board, I knew it was time for us to split. I developed a headache and convinced Cliff to take me home.

Returning to Mama's bedroom, I sat on the chair beside her bed. "You know, Mama," I said, trying to repress the fact that I'd wanted to wipe Cricket out myself when she'd rubbed up against Cliff, "there . . . uh . . . might be a reason for somebody to kill Cricket. You know, it could have been that Clarence took Cricket out on a date, things got rough, and he lost it. From the things Cricket said at Yasmine's party, she's had her share of rough dates."

Mama grunted. "Abe is still talking to Clarence. I suspect he'll get to the bottom of his story, see if he was out of town working like he said. You know, Simone, people saw the wild side of Cricket, but there was more to her than that."

I listened.

"You remember me telling you that I was at the hospital when Cricket gave birth to Morgan? Cricket had asked the nurses to call me. Even though her sister Rose was with her, she wanted me by her side. When I got to her, she grabbed my hand and held it as if she was holding on for dear life. 'I'm scared, Miss Candi,' she told me. 'Scared I'm going to die.' The poor child was so helpless, I almost wished I could have had that baby for her."

I smiled, knowing Mama meant what she said. She never could bear to see anyone suffer.

"You know, Simone, both her mother and father died in a car wreck when she was only two years old. Oh, she's got plenty of family to look after her, but she was a very lonely young woman. The day after Morgan was born, I visited Cricket at the hospital again. She confided in me that she'd deliberately stopped taking her pills and gotten pregnant because she wanted somebody to share her life with. She felt that now that she had given birth to Morgan, she would never feel alone again. That's why I know she was a good mother. I know she'd never deliberately mistreat her baby."

"There's something else bothering you, Mama, isn't there?" I asked.

"Yeah," she answered. "Something that's not related to Cricket's death, or Morgan. Before James left for work this morning, he told me that Midnight brought something home."

"That crazy dog is always bringing things here that don't belong to us, and—"

Mama interrupted. "Midnight brought home a baby's skull."

I shuddered. "Maybe he's been digging in somebody's cemetery," I said.

Mama pushed her tray toward me. "James is taking the skull to Abe for him to send it to Columbia to have it examined by the state forensic lab."

I picked up her tray and headed for the door.

"Somehow, I don't think that's where Midnight got that skull," Mama said, shaking her head. "No, I don't think Midnight visits cemeteries at all. . . ."

Mama is fifty-three. She works as a caseworker at the county's Department of Social Services. While many things that arouse the mind don't excite Mama, she becomes euphoric when her mind is deducing. Long ago, Mama decided that if she could get at the truth of a problem, she would have made her contribution to humankind.

Mama and I have been playing detective since I was a little girl. Our game has only two rules: First, we protect each other. Second, we can always count on the other being around to help when needed.

I put the breakfast dishes into the dishwasher, poured in the Cascade, and pushed the on button. That look in Mama's eyes told me that she had been bitten by what she called "the sleuthing bug." Cricket's murder and the skull Midnight had brought home would have her undivided attention until she found out the truth behind them.

By the time I was headed back into her bedroom, Mama was trying to stand up. I got to her side just in time to keep her from falling.

"Mama, you're supposed to stay in bed," I reminded her.

"We've got things to do," she insisted, leaning against me and pulling her nightgown over her head. She didn't say any more. Her silence told me that she was thinking. I helped her wash up and put on clean clothes. Finally, when she was sitting at her dressing table, she spoke. "You'll be here for a week. You can help me in and out of the car," she said.

"Mama," I asked, suddenly remembering Cricket's baby's bewitching eyes. "Is it hard to raise a child?"

Mama stopped combing her hair. "Simone, sweetheart, I believe that the secret to raising children is in doing three things: First, set the example for whatever you want them to be. Second, love them unconditionally. And, third, accept them for their own uniqueness."

"That's all to it?" I asked.

Mama smiled. "If you get that right, honey," she said, "most other things will fall into place."

CHAPTER
THREE

Mama and I stepped out on the front porch. Now the moisture in the morning's air was a warm drizzle, no more than a mist.

There was an odd expression on Mama's face as she slid into the passenger's side of my Honda. For a second I suspected that she was having second thoughts about being taken to the Cherry Ridge apartment where Cricket had been murdered, but I knew that if she was uncomfortable with the idea, she'd never admit it.

I put the key into the ignition and started the car, swung off Smalls Lane where my parents had built their ranch home years earlier. I pulled onto Highway 3 and headed east.

Mama was silent. I drove slowly but when she winced, I asked, "You okay?"

She nodded, slowly. "Yeah, but I suppose I should be home with my feet up."

"Let's go back," I urged.

Mama held up her hand. "No," she said. "Drive me to the Cherry Ridge Apartments. I'll stay in the car, you can bring the neighbors to me."

"Perhaps this trip wasn't the thing for you to do," I argued.

"I will be all right," she said firmly, determined.

The Cherry Ridge Apartments consists of two long brick buildings facing each other and separated by a promenade of a paved street. Each building has six apartments in it. Behind the complex is a small wooded area. The complex looks like an oasis in the middle of a forest. In the front of the building on the right there is a large Dumpster for tenants' garbage.

Everything was quiet. The only sign that death had visited the area was the yellow ribbon marking off the first apartment on the left side of the road.

I pulled up in front of the yellow ribbon. Nobody and nothing moved. Then, a screen door opened. A woman eased onto the small stoop of the apartment next to the one in which Cricket's body had been found. The door to Clarence Young's apartment was closed tight and padlocked.

Mama beckoned to the woman. "Koot," she called.

Koot Rawlins eyed Mama, then she walked toward us. I took a deep breath, remembering how difficult it was to be around this woman for long because her gas usually came from places other than her mouth.

Koot belched. "What you doing out here, Candi?" she asked, once she had propped herself against the Honda's front fender.

"I just heard about Cricket," Mama said.

"Pitiful," Koot said, between belches.

"What do you know about her?" Mama asked.

"Nothing," Koot answered. "Ain't seen nothing, ain't heard nothing."

"Was Cricket known to hang around these apartments a lot?" Mama asked.

Koot shook her head. "I ain't seen much of that gal around anyplace," she said.

I heard a noise behind me and glanced at my rearview mirror. A battered red car was pulling up into the complex.

"Oh, no," I moaned.

Mama nodded a greeting to Sarah Jenkins, Annie Mae Gregory, and Carrie Smalls as the red Buick LeSabre passed us and parked in front of my car. A small line formed at each corner of Mama's mouth.

By this time Sarah Jenkins, Annie Mae Gregory, and Carrie Smalls had gotten out of their car. Sarah Jenkins, her frail body draped in a white dress that seemed to be one continuous piece of cloth from her neck down to her ankles, tried to smile. It took all of Annie Mae Gregory's energy just to ease her large body out of the car and stand up on the pavement. Carrie Smalls, whose jet black hair swayed in the slight breeze, walked toward us briskly. Her two companions followed her.

"Candi," Carrie Smalls began, without acknowledging me. "How's those feet of yours doing?"

"I'm a little uncomfortable," Mama admitted.

"I'd better take you home—" I said, turning the key in the ignition.

"Before you go running off," Sarah Jenkins said to me, "I need to tell Candi about Cricket's baby."

"What about Morgan?" Mama asked.

"She's been stolen," Annie Mae Gregory answered.

I switched off the ignition.

Carrie Smalls took up the reporting. "We saw that deputy of Abe's come hurrying out of Kelley's Print Shop over on Main Street about an hour ago."

"Something up, I thought to myself," Sarah Jenkins continued. "Sure as I'm born to die, I said to Carrie and Annie, something is up for Rick Martin to be coming out of Kelley's in such a hurry."

"She was right," Annie Mae confirmed. "Sarah knew what she saw."

"I've got an eye for seeing things that ain't quite right," Sarah said proudly.

Carrie Smalls continued. "After Rick cleared out, we went inside and talked to Pete Kelley."

"I like Pete. He's always ready to talk," Sarah interjected.

Annie Mae Gregory took a deep breath, then spit the words out fast, as if to keep her two friends from cutting in. "Pete told us that Abe had sent Rick to his shop to make picture posters of Morgan Childs. Told us that nobody in either Cricket's family or that good-for-nothing boyfriend of hers, Timber, has seen that baby since yesterday morning, hours before somebody sliced up Cricket over there in Clarence Young's apartment," she said.

Mama turned to me. "Take me to Abe," she said, her voice anxious.

I started the car again. "We'll be by to see you later," Carrie Smalls promised as we pulled away from the curb.

The front door of the jail opens into a small foyer. On the left side there is a door that leads into a room which has one large desk, one small desk, two executive chairs, two file cabinets, a water cooler, a small table with a coffee urn on it, and four wooden chairs. This is the domain of Sheriff Abe Stanley and his deputy, Rick Martin.

On the other side of the foyer is a door that leads to three holding cells, residence for those who break Otis's laws.

"What's this I hear about little Morgan being kidnapped?" Mama asked, no sooner had she shuffled into Abe's door and sat down on one of his wooden chairs.

Abe Stanley, a man whose facial expression changes with his every thought, grimaced. "It's a fact, Candi," he said, almost apologetically. You see, the sheriff and Mama had developed a friendship that most of the time ensured Mama would get that

kind of information direct from him. The fact that
she knew about the murdered woman's missing
baby before he'd had a chance to call and tell her
himself seemed to embarrass him. "How did you
find out about it so quickly?" he asked.

"Sarah, Carrie, and Annie Mae," Mama answered.
"They saw Rick leave Pete Kelley's print shop. Pete
told them that you'd ordered posters to be printed of
Morgan to spread around the county because she's
missing."

Abe stuck a Camel in the corner of his mouth, but
he didn't light it. Earlier on, Mama had told him that
she couldn't take the smoke. "A couple of hours ago
Rose, Cricket's sister, came by here. She told me she
hadn't seen Morgan since yesterday morning when
Timber came and picked that baby up to take to his
mama's for a visit. So I called Timber's mama, Dollie
Smith. She told me that Timber came home around
ten o'clock yesterday morning and he didn't have
Morgan with him. Said he slept until around six,
then left. Said she asked him about Morgan and he
just said that Morgan was getting good care. Dollie
assumed Timber was talking about Cricket, so she
didn't ask him anything else about the baby. I told
Dollie to check with the rest of her family, to see if
Morgan was with one of them." He shook his head.
"Dollie called me back an hour ago. Nobody in her
family admits to seeing that child for at least two
weeks."

Abe slouched in his chair. "The way I figure it, that
baby is still alive, 'cause if she was dead we'd have

found her body alongside her mama's, don't you think so, Candi?"

Mama let out a breath, like she had been holding it, afraid. "I certainly do," she replied. "So, until we've got reason to believe otherwise, Morgan is alive and we've got to find her before—"

"Rose Childs told me," Abe cut in, "that after she got the word that Cricket had been knifed to death, she tried to get in touch with Timber but she couldn't reach him."

Abe took a book of matches out of his pocket, looked at it, then put it back in his pocket. "Candi, if you'd seen the room that poor girl was butchered in, you'd have thought you was in a hogs' slaughtering house. There was blood all over that place—floor, walls, bed, everywhere. Poor Cricket must have gone down fighting. I think she died on the rug, and her body was put on the bed later. She took five stabs with a butcher's knife, but they didn't kill her. Whoever did it must have gotten mad 'cause Cricket wouldn't die easily. He finally put his hands on her throat and squeezed it until she died."

Mama shuddered. "Was there blood in any of the other rooms in the apartment?" she asked Abe.

"All the other rooms in Clarence's apartment were undisturbed. In all my days as sheriff of this county, Candi, that bedroom is the worst crime scene I've ever seen. I can just imagine what that poor girl went through before she left this world."

"She didn't want to die," Mama said, her voice low, thoughtful. I remembered what she'd told me about how terrified Cricket had been of dying when she was in labor with Morgan.

"What evidence did you find in the bedroom?" Mama asked Abe.

"A few glasses, one with lipstick."

"Anything that might belong to a baby?" Mama asked.

Abe shook his head. "Nothing. Not even a pacifier."

"Then it's possible that Morgan wasn't in the apartment with Cricket after all."

A wrinkle creased Abe's forehead. "I'm thinking that the baby was with Cricket, that whoever killed her decided to take the child with him."

"Who would do a thing like that?" I asked.

"The person on the top of my list is Timber Smith, Cricket's boyfriend. I've got an APB out on him. Once I track him, talk to him, I'll have a better fix on the whole thing. Still, I guess I'd better put a call in to the State Law Enforcement people. I'm going to need help on this one."

Mama looked down at her watch, then stood up slowly. "Let me suggest that after Rick finishes putting up the posters of Morgan's picture all over the county, get him to talk to Timber's kinfolks. Perhaps they will tell him something about Timber's whereabouts that they wouldn't tell Rose."

"I'll do that," Abe agreed.

"Right now," Mama continued, "I'm going home and rest these aching feet. Tomorrow morning Simone will take me to a few places I need to visit, and to talk to a few good people who don't mind telling me things I need to know about Cricket and Timber."

When I got Mama back to the house, I gave her two Meprozine capsules and made her as comfortable as I could. Then I fixed lunch—chicken soup, grilled cheese, a diet cola, and a small bowl of ice cream. No sooner had she eaten, Mama fell asleep.

I sat in the family room, pushing the television remote control restlessly until the telephone rang. I wasn't too surprised to hear Yasmine's voice. She knew that I'd be with Mama for the week, and I'd expected her to call to see how Mama was doing.

"Thank goodness you're finally home!" Yasmine's voice was breathy, nervous. "I've been trying to reach you all morning."

"Why?" I asked. "What's happening in Atlanta?"

"I'm in Martin," Yasmine said. "I'll be at your mother's house in half an hour."

Before I could ask another question, she hung up.

When I peeked through the peephole and looked into Yasmine's eyes thirty-five minutes later, I was shocked. There was a harried look on her face. She wore no makeup, her hair was pulled into an untidy knot at the nape of her neck and tied carelessly with a scarf—this was not the way my girlfriend usually looked. I opened the door. Yasmine rushed past me and into the center of the family room. There, she stood looking in every corner like she couldn't make up her mind which direction she wanted to head. She wore light faded jeans, a plain white T-shirt, and a pair of black sling-back sandals.

"Girl, what is wrong with you?" I asked. "You look like you lost the fight."

"What?" she asked distractedly.

"Forget it," I said. I cleared my throat.

Yasmine looked at her watch. "I'm hungry," she said.

I rolled my eyes. "Want a sandwich?"

Yasmine made a shrug so small it was barely noticeable. "Yeah, a sandwich would be good."

A few minutes later Yasmine was holding a grilled cheese sandwich she wasn't eating and pushing around a mug of Ethiopian coffee that I'd brought to Mama from Caribou Coffeehouse in Buckhead. She stared down blankly at her food.

"Something on your mind? Something we need to talk about?" I asked. "You're not sick, are you?"

Yasmine looked at me, then broke eye contact. But not before I saw the tears in her eyes. "Where's Miss Candi?" she asked, again not answering my questions. Her behavior was starting to scare me.

"In bed, asleep."

"Simone," Yasmine whispered, "I'm pregnant!"

I stood up, walked to the counter, and poured myself a cup of the coffee. I felt disappointed. I knew Yasmine was a strong believer in the traditional family. She'd always argued that the husband should come first, then a house, and lastly children.

I took my cup and sat across from her at the table. "Girl, common sense could have prevented something like that from happening!"

"I took a home pregnancy test," Yasmine whispered. "It's positive."

"Take another one!"

"I've taken three. Simone, they were all positive." I shook my head. What could I say?

She reached into her pocket for a tissue, wiped her wet eyes. *"Simone, I'm going to have an abortion!"*

Her words came down on me like a ton of bricks. The thought of Yasmine having an abortion stirred an emotion, what I can only describe as a sensitivity to the delicacy of life—and suddenly I liked that feeling, I wanted to protect it, nurture it. I couldn't think of anything to say, words wouldn't come. When I did speak, I heard my voice as if it came from a distance. "Girl, don't even think about doing something like that. You could handle a baby—"

Yasmine stood up. She began pacing. Then she stopped in front of me and stared, a cold, dead-eyed look. "Girl, don't you know that a baby is like a chain around your leg? It keeps you in lock-down!"

"What?"

She made an ugly face. "There's no way I can have a baby now. And, Simone, I need you to go with me to the clinic."

I threw my hands up. "Oh, no . . . you've got to be kidding . . . ain't no way I'm going with you to an abortion clinic!"

Yasmine lowered herself into the chair, her head

so straight it looked like she had a glass of water on the top of it. "You're my best friend, Simone. You've got to go with me!"

"Because I'm your best friend, I won't help you do this!"

Her face stiffened. "How do you know what's right or wrong? Who made you my judge and jury?"

She was right. This was Yasmine's decision, not mine. And I knew my friend had not made her decision carelessly, whether I agreed with it or not. I took a deep breath, trying to take the edge out of my voice. "I'm not your judge. But I am feeling that having an abortion ain't the thing to do!"

Yasmine was silent. She sat chewing the inside of her cheek. After a while, she spoke. "Why are you so protective now? You ain't never cared about babies before . . . you always said you didn't have the maternal instinct!"

I shrugged. "I don't know," I replied. "I guess I saw a baby a few days ago that turned a switch on inside me," I said, remembering Morgan's angelic smile and thinking of how somebody had snatched her away and killed her mother. Where was that poor child now? "And my feelings tell me to care about the baby you're carrying. I'll help you with it, I promise!"

She waved a hand dismissively at me. "Yeah, right!"

"Listen, Yasmine," I said. "You can't—"

"You're making a decision without even thinking about it!"

The knot in my throat tightened. "Okay," I told Yasmine. "I'll think about what you want to do but—and I mean this—I ain't promising you that I'm going to go with you to an abortion clinic."

Yasmine didn't take her eyes off me. "When will you get back to Atlanta?"

"Next week," I answered her.

"Think about it for at least that long," she said, then began chewing her cheek some more.

"Don't get your hopes up," I said.

"I'll wait until you get back to Atlanta before I make an appointment at the clinic. You'll change your mind by then!"

I didn't say anything.

The tears shone in Yasmine's eyes again. "Simone, I can't do this by myself."

"What about Ernest? Have you told him?"

"No. And I'm not going to. I ain't having Ernest marry me 'cause I'm having his baby!"

"He might *want* to marry you!"

"A baby don't make a man stay, and in the case of a black man it'll make him leave faster!"

"Once he knows—"

"No!—I ain't having Ernest beat me down . . . I ain't gonna tell him, don't want him to know!"

"Girl, you're crazy! Ernest has got a right to know!"

"No, he doesn't!"

"Suppose he wants his baby?" I asked.

"I'll—" Yasmine stopped, thought, then said softly, "I'm only twenty-five. I can have other babies. Once

we're married, I'll give Ernest all the babies he can
take care of!"

"Suppose—"

"Simone, get real! Men ain't got feelings for babies
like women do!"

"Who told you that?"

"If you listened to the women whose hair I do
every week, you'd *know* it!"

"My father—"

"Mr. James is different. He's from the old school,
not like these men today! I've heard my clients tell
me how their man disappeared once they became
pregnant! It's the way things *are* nowadays!"

"Maybe you need to spend less time talking to
your clients and more time doing their hair!"

She glared at me. "I'm not telling Ernest and
neither are you!"

"And if I do?"

"I'll never speak to you again, Simone. You and I
have been girlfriends since before Ernest, before
Cliff. I know you ain't about to let something like
this come between us now!"

I ran my hand through my braids. "Yasmine," I
said, "you're supposed to have some sense . . . don't
do this thing to your baby!"

She made a funny sound in the back of her throat.
"Give it a week! Think about being in my shoes.
Then you'll see things my way."

I shook my head. "Believe what you want," I said,
deciding already that there was no way that I was
going to change my mind.

She stood and began walking toward the front door. Then she turned. "Simone," she said. Her voice cracked.

"Yeah!"

"Don't tell anybody what I've told you. Not even Miss Candi."

"I won't say anything," I promised.

She cocked her head, pulled on the neck of her T-shirt, then opened the door. "I ain't kidding. Don't mention it to your mama . . . I don't want Miss Candi thinking bad about me!"

"Mama isn't judgmental," I said. But I couldn't help but wonder what my mother would think if I told her that *I* was going to have an abortion.

CHAPTER

FOUR

The Covingtons are natives of Otis County. They own quite a bit of land, property that my great-great-grandfather obtained during Reconstruction. His oldest son was my great-grandfather, Ezekiel Covington. Great-grandpa Ezekiel's youngest and only living child was my great-uncle Chester. He had died six months earlier at the ripe age of ninety-nine.

Uncle Chester had quite a few children himself, since he'd buried three wives. It was his daughter, Agatha, however, who inherited Great-grandfather Ezekiel Covington's shrewd business sense. Cousin Agatha is a tall thin woman, with banana-colored skin. She has never married and, to my knowledge, has never wanted to. When you meet her she appears shy. But this is a deception. She is so astute in the handling of the Covingtons' land that you'd think she had a degree in business management.

It was Cousin Agatha's cleverness, along with a few encouraging words from Mama, that convinced Uncle Chester to give Agatha the power of attorney before he died. Cousin Agatha set up the Covington Land Company and had it incorporated, ensuring that our land would stay in the family for at least another hundred years.

Daddy's cousin, Fred Covington from Philadelphia, doesn't value land ownership the way Cousin Agatha does. As a matter of fact, Uncle Fred's philosophy is that land is good only for burying the dead. Money, he says, is for the living.

While Cousin Agatha doesn't agree with her first cousin, she was keen enough to know that she could use a little cash to fix up the old house she and Uncle Chester had shared for years. So she arranged to have the timber cut on the land, something that hadn't been done for decades.

Cousin Agatha shopped around for the best price and, when she'd finalized the deal, she wrote letters to the entire Covington clan, telling each one how much they could expect as their share of the proceeds of the timber sale.

For the past three weeks, the loggers had been cutting. Rain had stopped them temporarily, but once the sun came out, they'd pushed their trucks and saws further into the Covingtons' forest.

I don't know if Cousin Agatha suspected that the

loggers would try to cheat her or not, but she absolutely refused to leave her house while the timber was being cut all around her.

The first phone call I'd gotten after Yasmine left was from Cliff. He told me that things in L.A. were really getting bogged down. It seemed that Mrs. Campbell's appraiser came up with a greater value on their furniture than Mr. Campbell's. Mrs. Campbell had worked herself up into a fine state, telling Cliff she was going to get every cent of her husband's money.

Both Cliff's and Yasmine's problems had me in a sickening funk. So when Cousin Agatha called to tell me that she had cooked our dinner and that all I had to do was to come to her house and pick it up, I felt things were looking up a little.

I peeked into Mama's room. The Meprozine capsules had knocked her out; she would be asleep until either my father got in from work or I returned from Cousin Agatha's.

Happy that I didn't have to throw something together for the three of us to eat later, I got into my Honda and headed to Cousin Agatha's house near Cypress Creek.

It was a little after two-thirty when I pulled out of Smalls Lane. The rain had stopped; the sun was shining through the thickly tree-lined highway.

I popped in Nancy Wilson. Her tape, "A Lady with a Song," filled the car with her smooth and mellow voice. It was exactly what I needed on this trip. I felt depressed, or maybe sad . . . I don't know. Whatever my mood, Nancy's voice supported it.

The drive to Cypress Creek is along a twisting highway surrounded by acres of maples, silver-white birches, tall green pine and oak trees, and a thick undergrowth of shrubs. Every five or six miles, there is a sprinkle of farmhouses.

The strip is usually empty. The few cars that use it whisk through with no downtime. So when I glanced at my rearview mirror, I was surprised to see the dark blue Ford coming up fast behind me.

I slowed to let him pass. I wasn't in any hurry. Yasmine was on my mind. Her world is made up of cosmetics, fashion shows, and salon events. She is on the go so much, she barely keeps up with herself. My girlfriend is bright, the kind of woman who becomes more attractive the longer you know her.

Yasmine was a full-grown woman, I thought, capable of making her own decision, and I had no choice but to live with whatever she decided. I sighed, remembering that she hadn't asked my opinion. All she wanted was for me to go with her to the clinic.

I wrestled with that thought . . . to distance myself from personal involvement . . . to convince myself that I had to respect my best friend's decision. But the more I thought about it, the more intense my feeling against the abortion became.

And something else was bothering me. For years, I've had to defend not being maternal, not being a woman who thought the only way to be happy was to have kids. Now I was having to defend why I wanted to save an unborn child, so much so that I was risking my friendship with my best friend over it.

It was ironic that Yasmine's dilemma and the kidnapped Morgan were what it had taken to spark my maternal flame. Still, my conversion was real—I felt like I had finally become a sharer in the bond with all of my sisters—you know, that woman's thing that tells you to be a part of perpetuating the human race!

My hands gripped the steering wheel. "Yasmine would tell me to get pregnant without being married and have a baby myself, since I'm such a staunch opposer to her abortion!" I said aloud. That thought lingered. "I'm sorry, girlfriend," I said. "I don't care what you say, I'm not going with you to that clinic!"

This whole thing had me talking to myself. *Simone, get a grip*, I was thinking when from the corner of my eye I saw the driver of the blue Ford pick up speed. He put on his turn signal, then pulled out in front of me. As he drew even with me, he threw up his index finger like he was pulling the trigger of a gun.

The driver was black, middle-aged. His hair was woolly, long over the ears and combed back. His lips were uneven, his top one long and thin, his bottom lip fat. His beard was a scraggly thing that was in bad need of trimming. His complexion was leathery like he had spent a lot of time out-of-doors. The Ford slowed, then shot past me along the deserted road.

Once the Ford was out of sight, I was alone again. My unpleasant sight of the driver had made me a little uneasy, but with Nancy's song filling my car, I was beginning to relax. I thought of how Cliff would react if I was pregnant, what it would do to our relationship. That thought, and a nudge of the tightness still in my stomach, made me shiver. I lowered the air conditioner. "Pregnancy and babies," I whispered. "All of a sudden my world is filled with both!"

By that time I had noticed the blue Ford again. It was ahead of me, the driver moving less than twenty miles per hour. I slowed. As I did, he put on his signal to pull off to the side of the road, as if he had a flat tire. I drove past, looking for any sign of car distress. There was none. But as I pulled past, I noticed the baby's car seat strapped behind him.

The whole encounter took less than a minute and I wouldn't have thought any more about it except the Ford soon caught up with me again. This time the driver didn't pass. He was driving so close behind me that I thought he was going to ram my tail end. I glanced at the rearview mirror. The driver was staring at me unblinkingly. Something in the look on his face told me that this man would hurt me if he ever got the chance. And what I heard next made my heart jump into my throat. There was a thump and a fizz. One of my front tires had blown. I turned down the volume on the tape and took a deep breath. One of the things I've learned about panic is that it causes errors in judgment. Things happen fast, and because of the instinct for survival and the desire to get away to safety, thought usually follows action. *Be calm*, I told myself. *Think.* I knew how to change a tire. Cousin Agatha's house wasn't too far away. My eyes went back to the mirror. Just inches behind me, the blue Ford followed. The demented eyes of its driver just seemed to be waiting for me to stop my car. Flat tire or no, I kept driving.

The Ford stayed close behind me. I felt trapped, stupid. I kept staring back at the car inches behind me, fighting to stay calm, fighting to take deep, even breaths. *Think, think.*

The roadway was deserted, the silence eerily profound except for the rhythmic thump of my flat tire. There wasn't another car in sight. I took a deep, careful breath and with my left hand tight on the steering wheel, I opened the car pocket with my right hand. I examined the can of pepper spray I found there. Was it good? The last time I'd used it was during that affair in Bentley a year and a half earlier.

I glanced into my mirror again. The Ford was still inches behind me. But now, in the far distance, a white car was coming up fast behind both of us. My heart leaped. I whispered, "Thank goodness!" When I eased the Honda toward the shoulder of the road, the driver of the Ford immediately followed.

I switched off the car, checked to make sure that all of the doors were locked. A flock of crows, disturbed by our arrival, cackled and scolded, then flew off over the tall trees. I prayed.

The man in the Ford behind me didn't move. I was

beginning to wonder why he hadn't gotten out of his car and come toward me when I realized that he, too, had seen the approaching car . . . he was going to wait until it passed before he made a move.

As the white BMW neared, I flung open the door and jumped from my Honda. I ran into the middle of the highway, waving my hands frantically and screaming as loud as I could.

The driver of the BMW slowed his car. Two young men in their twenties and a young woman gaped out at me, confused.

"Help me!" I screamed. "Please help me!"

The young man who was driving stopped his car. He opened his window and said, "Calm down, lady . . . what's your problem?"

"My tire," I said. "I've got a flat tire!"

"Uh, you feel like changing a tire?" the driver asked his two passengers. The young lady in the backseat rose up, looked me in the eyes, then whispered something to the two men.

I felt the eyes of the man in the Ford boring straight into me. I pointed. "That man has been following me! If you won't fix my tire, at least give me a ride . . . Just don't leave me!" I begged.

The three people in the BMW looked toward the parked Ford. "Okay, lady," the driver said, as he swung his car in front of my Honda. "If you've got a tire jack, we'll change your tire!"

The man in the Ford shook his head. Then he turned the key in his ignition and pulled back out onto the highway. When he swerved past, I saw for the first time the baby who was strapped into the infant's seat.

The man had Cricket's baby in his car!

CHAPTER

FIVE

Yasmine's problem had stuck in my throat like a lump of scorched rice pudding; the guy who had Morgan added to that lump. Now the only thing I could taste was bile.

I'd planned to go back to Atlanta on Saturday. I'd concentrate there on influencing Yasmine not to have the abortion. After thinking about Cliff's problem with his client, Mrs. Campbell, I decided that whatever delay he'd have in getting back to Atlanta would allow me time to spend with Yasmine. Now, that cold-eyed turkey in the blue Ford had pissed me off in a way that made me want to stay in Otis long enough to help Mama not only to track down who had brutally murdered Cricket, but to find out who had kidnapped little Morgan. If, as I strongly suspected, the baby's kidnapper was the guy in the blue Ford, I'd take pleasure in personally throwing salt into his eyes.

By the time I'd picked up the food from Agatha and driven back home, a hodgepodge of emotions were surging through me. As soon as I walked into the house I'd intended to tell Mama that I'd spotted little Morgan, but I found her steadying herself, pressing one hand on the wall for support as she painfully made her way toward the family room. I waited until she was seated in the family room, her feet propped up on a stool. The expression on her face told me that she already knew I had something I wanted to tell her.

"You wouldn't believe who I saw," I began. No sooner were the words out of my mouth, however, than my father walked into the room. He pointed to the food on the tiled kitchen counter. "What's that?" he asked.

"Cousin Agatha sent dinner," I said, glancing at Mama. I suspected my father was thinking that while his cousin's cooking could never equal Mama's, it was definitely better than anything I could throw together. Whatever he was thinking, he pulled back the foil paper that covered the bowls. "Field peas, rice, corn bread, and fried chicken," he reported, then he shook his head. "I'll eat later." He turned and headed toward the front door.

"Mama, you wouldn't believe who I saw," I began again before we heard the door shut behind him.

Mama's stare was a big question mark.

"Morgan—I saw Morgan less than an hour ago," I told her.

Mama's eyes grew wide.

"I swear—when I was going to Cousin Agatha's house. On Highway Three, that winding road that dead-ends near the Cypress Creek road. Morgan was inside a blue Ford that some fool was driving."

I quickly explained what had happened to me on the highway. Then I told Mama, "That goon had such an angry look on his face, he made me sure that he would have tried something crazy if he could. Thank goodness those kids came by."

Mama studied my face. "Would you recognize the man if you saw him again? Or the car?"

"Of course I would," I said.

We were both silent, but it was a packed, thoughtful silence. Then the doorbell rang. The expression on Mama's face told me that she didn't want visitors.

After the third ring, I opened the door to Sarah Jenkins, Annie Mae Gregory, and Carrie Smalls.

The three women brushed past me and walked directly into the family room. To my surprise, Mama greeted them happily. When everyone was seated, Carrie Smalls eyed Mama grimly. "You feeling better?"

Mama smiled slightly. "Yes," she answered. "I guess I didn't realize how painful the removal of bunions could be."

Sarah Jenkins sniffed. "You should have asked me before you had it done, Candi. Couple years back I had a bunion, a callus, *and* a corn cut from *one* foot."

Mama said, "I'm sure that was some affliction."

"It's a fact," Sarah Jenkins said, proud of her ordeal. "Doctor had to break a bone in my foot just to set it straight again."

Mama nodded sympathetically, then she asked, "Did you ladies find out anything about Cricket's murder this morning when we left you at the Cherry Ridge apartments?"

Annie Mae Gregory's thick jaws wobbled. "We found out that Cricket was in some kind of scam that forced quite a few men in Otis to pay her money each week to keep her quiet."

Carrie Smalls folded her arms across her chest, and pushed her breasts up like balloons as she proudly added to their astonishing report. "Mattie Snipes told me her husband was paying Cricket fifty dollars a week to keep some kind of a secret from the deacon board of his church. Mattie said she for one was glad the hussy was dead. Now that fifty dollars of her husband's hard-earn money could go to her house, where it was suppose to be going all along."

"Heaven knows how many other men in Otis was dishing out money to that good-for-nothing Cricket Childs," Annie Mae Gregory continued smugly.

Mama gave the women a long, serious look, but she didn't make any comment. If the news about Cricket being a blackmailer surprised her, nothing in her face showed it.

Annie Mae Gregory continued. "The way I figure it, if Cricket had ten men whose secret she was keeping and each gave her fifty dollars a week, that's enough money for a heap of people to want to see that girl gone on to her reward, whatever torment as that may be."

Sarah Jenkins's brow wrinkled. "If I had a husband, and a hussy like that was making him give her money every week, I'd likely kill her *myself*. Course, that ain't no reason to steal her innocent baby. The Good Book did say, though, that your sins will go against your children. I suspect Abe will find that child Morgan out in somebody's field butchered up just like her no-good heifer of a mama."

At first I wondered why Mama wasn't responding to the news of Cricket's little scam. Then I realized that she probably knew somebody else who would know more about it than these ladies. "Did you know Cricket's mama or daddy?" Mama asked them.

Sarah Jenkins coughed.

"Sure did," Carrie Smalls answered. "Cricket's daddy's name was Archie Childs from Sugar Hill."

"You probably went to school with Cricket's mama, Barbara Williams," Sarah said.

Mama looked interested. Annie Mae Gregory shifted. Her body shook like a walrus trying to sit in a chair. "Barbara was stunted. Not five feet tall when she was full grown."

Recognition flashed in Mama's eyes. "She was bright-skinned, had thick lips?"

"That was Barbara, all right," Annie Mae Gregory said.

Mama nodded. "Barbara and I were in the twelfth grade together, and then—"

"She got knocked up," Carrie Smalls interrupted. "Archie Childs got Barbara Williams pregnant."

"She never graduated?" Mama asked.

"Naw, back then it was a shame for a girl to carry a child before she got married," Sarah Jenkins said. "Ain't like today, when getting knocked up without a husband is like dressing up in your Sunday best and strutting around town."

Now, I felt myself squirming uncomfortably. Sarah Jenkins's description of an unmarried pregnant woman wasn't exactly my vision of my friend Yasmine. And I knew that wasn't the way Yasmine saw herself.

Mama leaned forward. "Did Barbara marry Archie?" she asked.

"Not right then, not with that baby," Carrie Smalls told us. "That baby was dead when it was born."

Annie Mae Gregory raised her eyebrow. "No matter that the good Lord saw fit to take the child, Barbara didn't learn her lesson. She kept on fooling with Archie, and two years later, she was big as a watermelon again."

"Is that when they got married? When that baby was born?" Mama asked.

The three women nodded.

"How many more children did Archie and Barbara have?" Mama asked.

"Heap of them, eight in all," Sarah Jenkins replied. "That fool girl was made to have babies, and Archie must have known it from the first time he put his hands on her." She sighed in disapproval. "Cricket was the last baby Barbara had. Barbara and Archie were killed in a car wreck together. Cricket was in the car with them, but the Lord saved her, though I can't for the life of me understand why."

"The Lord works in mysterious ways," Annie Mae Gregory said.

"I suppose we should pay our respects to the Childs family," Mama said. And I knew from her tone of voice that one of the stops that she expected me to chauffeur her to would be to Sugar Hill where the Childs family lived.

"Talk to Cricket's oldest sister, Rose. Rose knows more about Cricket's scam than she saying, I'm sure of it!" Bitterness crept into Carrie Smalls's sharp voice.

Mama smiled thinly. "I know Rose well. She's a serious young woman, and if she's keeping something, she's got a good reason for doing so."

Carrie Smalls's voice grew even sharper. "Rose is the kind who likes to keep people out of her family's business. That's why she won't tell us anything."

I smiled, thinking that these three women didn't like being kept in the dark about *anybody's* business.

Suddenly a change came over Mama's face. She yawned. Her eyelids drooped. I knew she'd just gotten up from a nap, but now she seemed so sleepy she could barely stay awake. I assumed that she had had enough conversation with these three, and that she had something else she wanted to do more right now. So, I tried to help. "Mama, you'd better lie down and rest," I suggested.

Mama opened her lips, then closed them again.

Sarah Jenkins straightened her back. "Candi, you ain't been in your bed since you've been out and about this morning?" she exclaimed in horror. "When I had my foot operated on, it took me nearly six weeks to feel like getting around again."

Mama's face clouded. "I suppose I am a bit tired," she said, her voice soft and slightly weak.

Annie Mae Gregory, Sarah Jenkins, and Carrie Smalls stood. Five minutes later, they were gone. I locked the door behind them and set the security alarm, a system that Daddy had installed when there had been several break-ins on Smalls Lane. The only problem was that half the time we forgot to set it.

When I returned to the family room, Mama was looking out into her garden. She sat so quietly, I could almost hear the wheels in her head turning. I knew that she was trying to figure out this new information about Cricket. She was so sure that what she'd considered as a rough veneer only masked a very frightened young woman. Now, not only had she learned something new about Cricket's personality, but it opened up a Pandora's box of people with real reasons to murder Cricket, and to kidnap her child. "Simone," Mama finally said very quietly, "Cricket has a girlfriend that she hangs with. Her name is Sabrina Miley. I want to find Sabrina and talk to her tonight."

MIDNIGHT . . .
TWO

The path came to a tiny bridge that crossed a wide pond. The sun broke through the billowing white clouds; the water reflected the sky like a shiny mirror. The hum of blowflies feasting on a dead squirrel got Midnight's attention.

After a pause, he turned, and walked along to the straggly path that led deeper into the woods. The air was cool, and dark, because the tall trees filtered out most of the sunlight. Midnight stopped and watched a pair of woodpeckers flitter past his head; he let out an impatient yelp. A chipmunk dashed by. He raced after it, but tripped over the fat root of a maple tree and fell into a thicket of brambles.

Midnight stood and shook the dead leaves from his coat. He was deep into the woods now, a quarter of a mile along the path that would take him to the old house.

The dog made a noise, a howl that got caught in his throat.

Midnight sniffed, stretched his neck, and accepted what he suspected had happened long ago. He looked down the path, an air of resolution in his eyes as he walked toward the empty house, past the back porch, toward the graves.

CHAPTER

SIX

When Mama answered the ringing telephone, I heard the tiredness in her voice. But then she sat straight up in her chair. "Are you all right? . . . What happened? . . . Did you see it? . . . Is Abe all right?" she asked.

My heart took a loop. Something else serious had gone down. "What's the matter?" I asked.

Mama didn't answer, but stared at me.

When she put the phone on its receiver, I was standing at her side. "Would you please tell me what's happened?"

"James and Coal were standing in front of the courthouse."

"Yeah?"

"James said they heard a noise and looked toward

Smoak Street in time to see Abe and Rick in a high-speed chase after Timber and some other guy.

"Timber and his companion were driving a blue Ford, perhaps the very one that you encountered on the road to Cypress Creek." Mama breathed deeply. "You did say that Morgan was in a car seat . . . Did she look all right to you? I mean, did she look like she was being treated okay?"

"Now, Mama." I tried to sound more confident than I felt. "There's no reason to think that the man who ran off with Timber was the same one that tried to scare me. But, to answer your question, Morgan wasn't crying or anything."

Mama didn't say any more; she was thinking. I went down the hall to the bathroom, something that I should have done the minute I walked into the house. When I got back, Mama sat by the window staring into the garden again. I went over to her and began to massage her shoulders. I was about to tell her that I'd been thinking about spending another week with her in Otis when the key turned in the front door.

"James?" Mama called out.

"Yeah," Daddy answered as he stopped to key in the password on the security.

"Any news?" I asked, when he joined us.

Daddy shook his head. There was a resigned look on his face. "Abe didn't catch Timber and his buddy, if that's what you mean. Frankly, I'm putting my money on those guys being out of state in a couple of hours."

"Did you see a car seat in the backseat of the blue Ford that Timber and his friend were driving?" Mama asked.

"A what kind of seat?" Daddy asked, looking puzzled.

"A child's car seat," Mama replied.

"Honey, things happened so fast. And, to be truthful, I wasn't looking for no child's car seat."

"Why would Timber run from Abe when all the sheriff wants to do is talk to him?" Mama asked softly, like she was talking to herself.

" 'Cause he's guilty," Daddy replied.

"If he's guilty," I said, "why is Timber hanging around Otis, driving in the heart of town in broad daylight? Why hasn't he skipped town long before now?"

" 'Cause he's stupid," Daddy said. He headed for the kitchen.

Mama sighed. "There are so many questions with so few answers."

Midnight started barking.

"Simone, girl," Daddy called back to me accusingly from the kitchen, "I bet you didn't feed my dog!"

"No, dear father," I answered, without bothering to give him an excuse.

Daddy looked in the family room and grinned; he knew that I knew his statement was nothing but a friendly jab.

"Okay, be that way," he said as he walked toward the back door. "Midnight won't suffer, 'cause I'll feed my own dog." Midnight kept barking. "I'm coming, boy," Daddy said.

When Daddy hollered a few minutes later, I ran. My father was on his knees in front of his dog, gaping down at the grass. It took only a moment for me to understand his bewilderment.

Midnight stood wagging his tail and looking pleased to have deposited another tiny skull at my father's feet!

CHAPTER
SEVEN

At nine-thirty, Mama and I were sitting in my Honda, which was parked under the canopy of an old oak tree on Elm Street. Directly in front of us was a shanty. Wooden-framed with four rooms, it was painted red. This was the third of six that are lined side by side in a single row on the street. Townspeople call the area the Redline.

The June night sky was clear, the quarter moon crisp overhead. Mama sat on the backseat with Sabrina Miley, who wore a light pink robe and whose hair was rolled in fat curlers. "Sabrina, what did you get Cricket caught up in?" Mama asked pointedly.

When Sabrina didn't answer Mama right away, I looked back, but the only thing I could make out of the young woman was a silhouette. "I—I ain't got

Cricket into anything that she didn't want to get in," she finally answered defensively.

Mama must have taken note because when she spoke again, her voice was softer, lower. "You're absolutely right. Cricket was a big girl. She did exactly whatever she wanted to do."

Sabrina's tone hardened. "People like to think that once a person is dead, they never done anything wrong while they were alive. I know better than that. Far as I'm concerned, what you do when you're alive don't change just 'cause you die."

"I agree with you," Mama said.

"My daddy beat me and my mama *almost* up to the day he died," Sabrina continued. "At his funeral the preacher said he was headed for heaven. But my daddy was mean and evil when he was alive and I ain't got no reason to believe that changed once he died."

"I see what you mean," Mama said, her voice even softer.

"Cricket was my friend 'cause we liked the same things, the same kind of people," Sabrina continued.

"That may be true, but it's possible that there's one person, perhaps somebody you and Cricket liked a lot, who is a killer," Mama told her gently.

Sabrina made a short nervous sound that I surmised was meant to be a laugh. "N—none of our friends would hurt Cricket."

"Somebody stabbed Cricket five times, then choked her to death. There is a *dangerous* man walking around in Otis."

"Nobody me or Cricket fool with is like that."

Mama took a deep breath. "Sabrina, if one or more of your friends, someone who was also one of Cricket's *special* friends, were the kind to get rough while they were playing, who would they be?"

"Th—the kind of friends Cricket and I played with didn't get too rough," Sabrina sputtered.

"Okay, then if one of your friends got angry because you threatened to tell a secret that he didn't want told, who would he be?"

Sabrina drew a shuddering breath. She didn't answer.

Even softer, Mama said, "The monster who killed Cricket is loose in Otis, Sabrina. And he might not be done yet."

"I don't like calling people's name," Sabrina insisted stubbornly. "Some people are willing to pay a lot of money for their name not coming up at the wrong time."

"Sabrina, please," Mama continued, "there's a killer walking around Otis. If he was a friend of Cricket's, he might be your friend, too. And if he did what he did to Cricket, you might be the next one on his list to hurt."

Sabrina cleared her throat. Still, she didn't answer.

"I won't mention you gave me the name if that's what you're worried about," Mama pressed. "I know how valuable keeping a secret can be."

"Miss Candi, I ain't one for accusing anybody falsely. But if you promise to keep this between me and you, the names of Joe Blake, Sonny Clay, and Les Demps come to mind."

"Joe Blake, Sonny Clay, and Les Demps," Mama repeated.

"Like I said, I ain't fingering nobody. All I'm admitting to telling you about them is that when they die, they ain't going to heaven."

"One more thing—" Mama added, as Sabrina opened the car door to step outside. "Would any of these men do any harm to Cricket's baby?"

Sabrina looked back toward Mama. Coldly, she said, "I don't know nothing about that baby—except Cricket told me once she thought Timber might steal Morgan from her and give her to his other woman."

It was ten o'clock the next morning. Billowing white clouds did nothing to protect from the sweltering June heat.

Midnight stretched out on our front porch in luxurious sleep, breathing rhythmically, his shiny black coat gleaming.

I remembered the day that my father had allowed this full-grown jet black dog to become a part of our lives. Six months ago, the dog had showed up on our doorstep, hungry and sick. He'd been so thin you could see his bones through his fur. Daddy fed the stray, then he took him to Dr. Claims, the town's only veterinarian.

Mama insisted that notices be posted all over the neighborhood, in case the dog's owner wanted him back. Three weeks later, when no one had responded, my father was convinced that he and this dog were destined for each other.

Daddy christened him Midnight. Then he built him a house and put it in the farthermost corner of the backyard. Midnight got chained to it so that he wouldn't damage Mama's carefully manicured yard of trees, shrubs, and flowers. While the dog was recuperating, things worked fine.

Once Midnight was healthy again, however, he began to bark. Continuously. It took my father only a few days and noisy nights to realize that his new dog was a rambler, an explorer, unaccustomed to and very unhappy about being in lock-down.

Reluctantly, Daddy let him run free, fretting silently that the dog wouldn't return. The first night Midnight came home dragging our neighbor Mr. Banks's smelly work boots, boots that Mrs. Banks wouldn't let inside of their house. Mr. Banks took his boots off on his back porch every evening, then, the next morning, he'd put them on again. Midnight changed all that. I think that Daddy was so glad that the dog came back home that he didn't realize Midnight felt his retrieving efforts had been rewarded when my father patted him on the head. When, the next day, Midnight brought Daddy Mr. Banks's boots again, Daddy just bought Mr. Banks another pair of boots. After that, Mr. Banks took off his new boots inside his garage, not on his back porch.

Midnight brought home sheets, towels, underwear. Each time my father cheerfully compensated the owners for their losses. Once, when I suggested to Daddy that he was training Midnight to steal, he laughed and told me, "Simone, a Labrador retriever is *supposed to retrieve!*"

But now, the tables had turned. Midnight had brought home two tiny skulls, the first of which had already been sent to the state forensic lab for examination. The look in my father's eyes suggested that his feelings about his dog's thieving habit were changing.

This hot summer morning, Mama had decided to wear a brown cotton skirt and a yellow blouse that complemented her candied brown complexion. Her beauty was marred by the pained intake of breath she made when I helped her into the passenger's side of the Honda.

Our first stop was to take this latest skull to Sheriff Abe's office. Mama had already telephoned Abe to arrange for the skull to be sent to the same laboratory in Columbia where he'd sent the first one.

As for me, no matter what was going on with Midnight's skulls, Morgan, Cricket, or Timber, thoughts of Yasmine kept meandering through my mind like a lovesick song. I still didn't know what I was going to say that would make her change her mind.

When Mama and I got to the sheriff's office, a cloud of cigarette smoke hung heavily in the air. The ashtray on the desktop in front of Abe was full.

"That Timber is as slippery as a catfish," he told us.

As usual, Sheriff Abe fumbled out a cigarette and stuck it between his lips, but he didn't light it.

"Have you heard anything about the whereabouts of little Morgan?" Mama asked as she sat in one of the wooden chairs.

Abe shook his head. "No, I'm afraid I haven't."

"Not one of Timber's kin has got the child?"

"I had Timber's mother, Dollie, call every one of her relatives all over the United States. Nobody owned up to seeing or hearing about Timber or Morgan in the past two weeks."

Mama took a deep breath. "What about Cricket's murder?" she asked. "Have you learned any more?"

"Cricket's fingerprints were on one of the glasses in the apartment. We know for a fact that Timber's prints are on the other glass because I had Timber in my jail a couple of weeks ago. He got drunk and I had to haul him in for trying to beat Cricket. Rick had the smarts to take his fingerprints then. We got a match off one of the glasses."

"So Timber and Cricket were in the room, but we still don't know if they were there at the same time. What about the blood?"

"Most of it was Cricket's blood. But there was somebody else's blood, too, although we haven't identified who that person is as yet. Once we get a chance to talk to Timber, we'll have a better chance of knowing whether it was his blood."

Mama reached into her purse and handed Abe a

piece of paper. "I've got three other names I want you to look at."

The sheriff read the names of Joe Blake, Sonny Clay, and Les Demps. He leaned forward.

"These are just names," Mama contended, "nothing more. It would be good if you could talk to these men, see what you can learn from each. Please, Abe, be discreet."

Abe's eyebrows rose. "How did their names come to you? What these fellers got to do with Cricket or her missing baby?"

"Cricket knew these men well," Mama answered. "Perhaps too well. By the way, did you find out who owned the blue Ford that you chased with Timber and friend inside of it?"

"The car was registered to Koot Rawlins," Abe said, "but she ain't seen it in almost six months. Her sister's boy, JC Bates, sold it to a feller named Warren for five hundred dollars. Koot showed me a receipt. She said she signed the title over to this Warren, but I suspect he never bothered to change the tags. From Koot's description of this feller Warren, along with what Rick and I saw of him, we've concluded that he is the one we spotted with Timber driving through town."

"I'm going to visit Rose, Cricket's sister, to see what she knows about Timber and his other women," Mama told Abe. "It might be that one of them has got Morgan holed up at her place."

"If you find that baby, you let me know right away," Abe said. "As for that Timber, I've got an APB out all over the Southeast for him and his buddy Warren."

"Have you gotten the report from Columbia on that first baby's skull that James's dog brought to our house?"

"Yeah," Abe nodded. "It's right here." He pulled a paper from the stack in front of him and handed it to Mama. "Course I ain't had a chance to do anything with it. Ain't even had a chance to alert people to Midnight digging in their cemeteries."

I smiled, but Mama wasn't amused. "Midnight didn't get that skull from any cemetery," she snapped, then opened the small box and unwrapped its contents, carefully placing it on Abe's desk.

Abe stared down at the second skull. "Lord, where *is* that dog digging?"

"Midnight is trying to tell us something," Mama insisted. "Nobody seems interested in listening to him but me." She read the report Abe had given her. After a few moments, she looked up. *"The baby was about four months old when it died!"*

"How can they tell that?" Abe asked.

I answered him. "I know from working with the forensics who help my boss get ready for his trials that they can tell from bones a victim's age, sex, race, and height. Sometimes, they can even tell the type of diet."

Mama frowned.

"Was there trauma to it?" I asked.

Mama looked down at the report again. "No, no trauma . . . Abe, there's something very wrong going on. I know you've got your hands full with Cricket's murder, and poor Morgan missing, but I need your help on this, too. Please, get the message out about these skulls. See if anybody knows where Midnight might be digging."

Abe sighed. "I'll get to it soon as I can," he promised Mama.

CHAPTER

EIGHT

An hour later, we were near the Coosahatchie River bridge, three miles south of Otis. Mama touched my arm, then motioned for me to stop the car just before we crossed the bridge. I tapped the brakes and pulled to the shoulder.

"Why do you want me to stop?" I asked.

"Those two women on the bridge," she replied. "One is Birdie Smiley. I haven't talked to her since that incident in Winn Dixie. I need to see how she is feeling."

Thick pines stretched their branches on each side of the highway. On the other side of the bridge, parked a few yards away from the two women, was a tan Chevrolet station wagon. To our right, directly across the highway, was a plowed soybean field with an oasis of woods behind it. Except for the sound of birds in the trees, the area was quiet, idyllic.

The driver of a green pickup truck stared at us as he drove by. No doubt he was wondering why we were parked. Mama waved, nodding in assurance that we didn't need help.

The sound of two crows who sat on the rail in front of the bridge's precipice drew my attention. The larger shuffled toward the road, then took to flight, its plumage shining in the sunlight. The other lifted its wings, as if it felt threatened. It moved its dark head from side to side, then stretched its neck and cawed. The ugly sound ricocheted off the trees. But before it died away, the second bird flew away, too.

The two women who stood on the bridge seemed oblivious to us. "What's Birdie and that other woman doing on the bridge?" I asked.

"Fishing," Mama answered. "James tells me that good-size fish flow from the river into this creek."

"Why don't we talk to Birdie later?" I suggested. "I want to get on to Rose's house. I'm anxious to find out what other women Timber was going with."

"I want to know if one of them is hiding poor Morgan, too," Mama said. "But give me a minute to speak to Birdie, Simone. Get out and ask her to come over here."

I nodded. Outside the car, the smell of grain was heavy in the summer air. As I walked up to Birdie, I recognized her companion as Koot Rawlins. A look passed between them, something said without being said. I told them that Mama was sitting in my car, and because of her foot surgery, she couldn't come down. She wanted to speak to Birdie, I said.

Birdie Smiley looked toward the tan station wagon before she spoke. "I suppose we should speak to Candi," she said placidly. She pulled in her fishing pole. Koot Rawlins whispered something underneath her breath, then belched and pulled her pole up, too.

When we reached the car, Mama had opened her door. Tiny beads of sweat stood on Koot's forehead. She leaned on the passenger's side of the Honda. Birdie stood directly behind her.

"Candi, how are you doing?" Koot asked, glancing down at Mama's feet.

"Pretty fair," Mama replied, fanning. "Course I never thought that it would be so hard for me to get around," she admitted.

Koot swiped at a fly, her eyes fixed on Mama's face. "Fact is, I didn't know you had had your feet cut on until Sarah, Annie Mae, and Carrie told me."

Mama looked surprised.

"Don't you remember? Soon after you and that daughter of yours drove up to the apartments yesterday, they came to see where Cricket got killed, too," Koot explained. "Sarah told me that you wouldn't be getting around for quite a while."

"Sarah is right," Mama admitted. "The fact is that I wouldn't be able to get out at all if it wasn't for Simone. I talked her into driving me to Cricket's sister's house."

Birdie grimaced. "If you were heading to Rose's house, what you doing out here?" she asked, staring down at Mama.

"I wanted to ask you how you are feeling. I hadn't seen you since Saturday. You know, when you were holding little Morgan."

"I've learned my lesson," Birdie answered. "I ain't got no business taking care of a baby."

"So, you are feeling better?" Mama asked, her voice concerned.

Birdie's eyelids fluttered. She seemed very careful not to look at Koot. "Isaiah promised Abe he'd make sure I take my pills like I'm supposed to."

Koot belched.

When Mama spoke again, she'd changed the subject. "What happened to Cricket," she said thoughtfully, squinting into the sunlight, "is horrible, and I aim to find out who killed that young woman so spitefully. But what concerns me more is what's happened to her little girl, Morgan. . . ."

Koot's eyes widened. She looked from Mama to Birdie.

Birdie Smiley made a tiny sound in her throat. The look on her face was nothing like the disoriented expression she'd had in the grocery store five days ago, before Cricket's murder—today, Birdie wasn't confused at all. "Ain't nothing happened to that child. Some of Cricket's people probably got that baby," she said, politely but firmly.

Mama looked doubtful. "From what I hear,

Cricket's kin ain't owning up to having Morgan. And it just doesn't make sense for anybody to hide the fact that they've got the child."

Koot's eyes narrowed. "Why would anybody else but Cricket's people want that hollering child? I don't see no reason for all the fuss about a child—some of Cricket's people got her stored away someplace so that people can make a fuss over her gone missing." Her voice was very, very angry.

Nobody spoke.

Koot cleared her throat. She shook her head as if to get her thoughts in order. "I—I don't know," she said, folding her arms under her breast, and sticking out her chin. "Tell Abe that little Morgan is with some of Cricket's people, and that will be the end of that!" Koot opened her mouth as if she was going to say more. She looked at Birdie and decided against it. For a few moments, there was nothing but the sound of the crows to break the stillness.

"Are you ready to get out of here?" I asked Mama.

But Mama had a curious glint in her eyes. "I promise you one thing," she said softly, looking into Koot's eyes. "I'm not going to stop until I personally see that little baby with Cricket's people."

Koot belched, but didn't respond. The silence was becoming uncomfortable so I slid into the driver's seat and said to Mama, "Let's go."

Mama nodded, closed her door, and said goodbye to the two women politely. I turned the key in the ignition, patted the gas, and eased onto the road.

We were finally going to Sugar Hill to visit the dead woman's sister, Rose. Birdie and Koot stood by the side of the road, staring and silent.

The air conditioner had somewhat cooled the car when I asked Mama, "You don't buy Koot's theory that Morgan is with Cricket's people, do you?"

Mama shrugged.

"My money is on that goon who was driving the car on Cypress Creek road. And he wasn't any kin to Cricket," I continued.

"How do you know that?" Mama asked.

"Mama, be for real!" I snapped, not wanting to believe that Koot was right that Cricket's people had Morgan hidden away.

"Simone, calm down," Mama said. "I'm not saying that Morgan is with any of Cricket's people."

"It doesn't make sense for Cricket's relatives to be hiding Morgan. If, for instance, that baby saw her mother being killed, she wouldn't be able to identify the murderer," I pointed out.

Mama nodded thoughtfully. "I'm thinking about Carrie Smalls's suggestion that Rose is holding something back." She paused. "If that is true, we can't leave Rose's house until we've found out if what she's not telling us has anything to do with Cricket Childs's death or Morgan's whereabouts."

CHAPTER
NINE

The fresh pork was seasoned with onion, garlic, and green pepper. . . . I knew, because its smell reminded me of how Mama cooked fresh neck bones for an hour before she added cleaned, cut collard greens.

The aroma of what Rose was cooking sashayed through the door of her little kitchen, meandered to the front of the mobile home, and drifted on the wind until it passed the huge oak tree, the rosebush with red blossoms that had been planted in the middle of the swept yard, and the hedge of wild-flowers that stood between the trailers. The scent of the pork landed at my Honda's window.

I don't know how this area became known as Sugar Hill. Brothers, sisters, aunts, uncles, and a few

cousins live in the fifteen mobile homes that sit together in a semicircle. The first trailer, the green-and-
white double-wide, belonged to Rose Childs.

Rose's unpaved driveway arched at the left and
ended at the rear of her mobile home. Mama pointed
toward a small area surrounded by a chain-link
fence in the field directly behind the trailer. "I've
never noticed that cemetery before," she admitted.
"Take a look at it before I call Rose."

I got out of the car and walked up to the compact
enclosure. The cemetery site was tidy. The grass had
been recently mowed. There were no flowers. The
gate opened easily. When I stepped inside the fence,
I got the feeling that I'd entered a sanctuary. There
was the normal stillness of death here, but there was
something else, too.

Each of the twelve small headstones carried the
name of a child, an infant who had died within nine
months of its birth.

"Mama!" I cried out. "This is a babies' graveyard—
It might be where Midnight has been digging."

"Does it look like a dog has been digging about?"
she called back. She sounded skeptical.

She was right. The grass was undisturbed. There
was nothing to suggest Midnight had been digging
here. "I guess this is not the cemetery where Midnight got his skulls," I admitted, disappointed. I
fanned at the swarm of gnats that my perspiration
had attracted.

The back door of the green-and-white trailer
opened and the screen door slammed shut. "Yo-ho,

what you doing there!" Rose Childs protested loudly as she walked from the door of her trailer. She was a little woman, shorter than her dead sister Cricket. She wore a pale yellow dress, one that had been washed many times. Her hair was pulled back from her broad, moon-shaped face with a black elastic headband.

I headed back to Mama. Rose and I reached the car at the same time. Her thick lips pouted. "What you doing out there?" she asked, her angry eyes glaring at me.

Before I had a chance to answer, Mama replied, "I've come to pay my respects for the loss of your sister, Rose. You have to forgive me for not getting out sooner. You see, I've had an operation on my feet and I can't get around—"

The look on Rose's face changed instantly from annoyance to sympathy. "Lord, Miss Candi," she exclaimed, "you don't need to be out here with cut-up feet. Come on in and let me prop them up for you."

Mama, who had taken a handkerchief from her purse, wiped the sweat from her face. "I appreciate that," she said.

And so Rose Childs and I helped Mama inside the trailer.

"I'm sorry about Cricket's death," Mama began once she was comfortably sitting on the sofa inside the trailer and sipping from the glass of iced tea Rose had given her. "I can't imagine who in Otis would have done such a terrible, terrible thing."

Rose's eyes brimmed with tears. "Cricket was

brazen and did things she ought not have done, but she didn't deserve to die like that," she told Mama.

"Do you have any idea who could have attacked her?" Mama asked.

"No." Rose's voice was so low and faint we almost didn't hear her.

But Mama nodded thoughtfully. And once again she changed the subject. "I've never noticed that cemetery. Tell me about it."

"It's been there almost twenty-one years," Rose answered, almost too quickly.

I could see that Rose's reaction had an effect on Mama's thoughts.

"Everyone who's buried in that cemetery is a child, a baby," I pointed out, thinking that this was the way Mama wanted the conversation to proceed.

Rose nodded. "My grandmother delivered all those babies herself."

"It's odd that they're buried in her cemetery and not with their own families."

Rose looked away. "I suppose . . ." she said. There was a slight tremor in her voice.

Mama smiled compassionately. "Is there a story behind that cemetery, Rose?" she asked in a tone I knew was meant to get Rose to feel close enough to share something that might be personal.

Rose didn't answer. She sat as if mistrusting, now glaring at us. I couldn't help but think that this young woman was smart. She'd quickly figured out that Sarah Jenkins, Annie Mae Gregory, and Carrie

Smalls were looking for information from her about her sister's murder for distribution throughout the county. Now, she was trying to decide whether Mama and I had the same motive.

Mama leaned forward. She touched Rose's clasped hands. "If there is a story behind your cemetery, I'd like to hear it," she said, her voice low and gentle.

When Rose didn't speak, I knew Mama's next strategy. She'd want us to sit quietly and allow a feeling of trust to grow in the room without words. Rose's body tightened like she was feeling something terrible. A painful look swept across her face. Finally, her shoulders relaxed a fraction and she said edgily, "My grandmother, Lucy Bell Childs, was a midwife. That's all there is to that cemetery."

I believe Mama and I reached the same conclusion at about the same time: Rose Childs wasn't going to tell us any more.

But Mama gave Rose a long, serious look. "Rose, I've got to ask you this and I want you to be honest with me."

Rose's lips thinned.

Mama waited for a moment before she continued. "Does anybody in your family have little Morgan hidden away?" she asked frankly.

Rose didn't blink. But she spoke in a confused voice, as if she couldn't believe Mama's question. "No! Nobody in my family knows what has happened to Morgan. But—" She stopped.

Mama pressed, "But what, Rose?"

Rose sighed. The sound seemed to come from somewhere deep inside of her little body. "Our whole family is praying for that baby—day and night, we're praying that the Lord will keep that child safe."

Mama frowned. When she did, it confirmed my own thoughts—something in Rose's voice betrayed that she was scared. Did she suspect her family's prayers *wouldn't* be answered? Or did she know it?

Mama touched Rose's hand again. "You sound like you know something more than you're saying," she said softly.

But again Rose stubbornly remained silent.

A slight look of exasperation crossed Mama's face, but it was brief—I really don't think Rose saw it. "Rose," Mama said, "I want to help you. I really want to help you."

Rose's hands trembled, but the rest of her body became rigid. It was as though if she moved, she feared she'd break. "There are wicked people in this world, Miss Candi," she whispered. "People who do evil things to innocent little children."

"You know those kinds of people?" Mama asked.

Rose didn't answer.

"I want to find Morgan," Mama said. "If you don't have her, perhaps you can help me find her."

Rose still didn't say anything.

"I'm thinking," Mama now said, "that Timber might have taken Morgan to stay with one of his other girlfriends. Did Cricket ever mention that she suspected Timber of messing with anybody else?"

Rose's body loosened. "What?" she asked, as if she was coming out of a trance.

"Did Cricket ever tell you that she suspected that Timber might steal Morgan and give her to another one of his girlfriends?"

Rose shook her head. "Cricket never thought—" Rose's voice trailed away. Then she sat fixed again, like she was determined that she wasn't going to talk freely.

Compassion was clear in Mama's face. I suspected since she was having her own pain, it was easier for her to identify with Rose's. "I don't think little Morgan is dead," she said gently. "Somebody in Otis has kidnapped Morgan and is hiding her. And Timber knows that she's here. It's the only reasonable explanation for him to be still hanging around Otis if he did in fact kill Cricket."

"Timber loved his baby, all right," Rose whispered.

"We've got to find Morgan before it's too late, before whoever has her takes her away from Otis," Mama continued. "If you know anything that can help me, anything at all—"

Rose looked like a little girl, scared of a particular villain. "Miss Candi," she said through choked tears, "I don't know where Morgan is at." She sounded confused, like she didn't understand the connection between Cricket's terrible murder and poor Morgan's kidnapping.

Mama decided not to push for more information. She gestured for Rose to join her on the sofa. But instead, Rose kneeled on the floor beside her. She threw her arms around Mama and began sobbing uncontrollably. "Don't you worry yourself none," Mama whispered, holding Rose gently in her arms. "We'll find Morgan, I promise—we won't stop until we find her!"

TEN

Mama had to spend all day Thursday in bed—her poor feet were very sore and swollen. A complete day of total bedrest was absolutely necessary.

As Mama ate the breakfast I'd brought her the next morning, the look on her face was distant, like she'd spread pieces of some puzzle in front of her mind's eye. The last thing she'd said before I left her to take her tray to the kitchen was, "Where *is* Morgan Childs?"

I shrugged and didn't answer. I knew the creep who'd tried to scare me on Cypress Creek road had Morgan and I knew that his motives weren't fatherly.

I cleared the table and stacked the dishwasher. The smell of Irish cream coffee, the second pot of the morning, filled the sunny room. It was peaceful and I felt glad to be home, glad to be with Mama when she needed me. I jumped when I heard the doorbell ring. It was a long siren like somebody's finger had gotten stuck on the bell. Once before I'd heard that kind of a desperate ring: That incident ended with Mama almost being killed. That memory made me swear to myself and peek through the door's peephole before I swung it open.

He was standing on our doorstep. Thirty-five, woolly hair, long over his ears, combed back. Lips uneven, the top long and thin, the bottom fat and pulled down by a scraggly beard. His complexion was leathery like he'd spent a lot of time outdoors. He wore a pair of faded jeans, a dingy white T-shirt, and a pair of old Reebok sneakers. I didn't need to see more. I remembered this creep's every detail, especially his unblinking, cold stare. Out on the Cypress Creek road, it had almost scared me to death. I stiffened when he pressed the doorbell again.

This had an odd feel to it; it was like fate had given me a second chance to cop the creep. *You must be tripping if you think you're going to get to this black woman*, I thought. I turned away from the peephole and headed for the kitchen. The instructor of a rape defense class I'd once attended told us that anything sprayed in an attacker's eyes would stop him cold. I was looking for a can of aerosol spray. These were one pair of nasty eyes I wanted closed.

The bell rang a third time. I pushed cans around in the cupboard. Finally, I spotted the oven spray. *This will end that cold stare,* I thought as I headed back for the door.

But when I got there, the creep wasn't on our porch anymore. I cracked the front door wide enough to see him walking toward the blue Ford that was parked in our driveway.

Midnight came tearing up the driveway. The man stopped and stared at the attacking animal. Midnight barked and leaped at him. The big black dog threw himself on the man, rearing up with his forepaws on his chest. The creep patted Midnight's head. The dog barked and wiggled and licked his face.

I stood with my can of oven spray in hand, speechless.

"Good to see you, boy," the man said. I was shocked; his voice was actually gentle. He began walking toward his car, Midnight following close at his heels. The stranger patted the dog again. Midnight wriggled with joy. Moments later, the blue Ford had pulled out of our driveway into the street.

I memorized his license number. But not before I noted that the infant carrier was no longer in the backseat.

"Simone," Mama hollered. "Who was at the door?"

I didn't answer her; I was thinking that it'd never crossed my mind that I'd see this scab at my own house.

Mama called again. "Simone, who was at the door?"

I hurried into her bedroom. "You won't believe this. You remember I told you about the guy who threatened me on the Cypress Creek road?"

Mama nodded.

"The creep who had Morgan in the backseat of his car," I added enthusiastically.

"Yes, Simone," Mama said patiently.

"He just rang *our* doorbell."

"Are you sure?" Mama asked.

"He was driving the same car— This time," I said proudly, "I've got his license number. Call Abe, Mama. Get him to check it out for us." I lifted up the receiver and dialed the sheriff's number, then handed Mama the telephone.

A cloud passed over Mama's face. Without speaking, she put the phone down on its receiver.

"You don't believe me?"

"Simone," she said, her tone gentle, practical. "Give yourself a minute to calm down. Then we'll talk about what just happened."

I slumped down in the chair next to Mama's bed. My heart raced; I was so pissed I felt a little dizzy. A ripple ran across the bedroom window, a breeze from the vent of the air conditioner.

Mama's voice was soft. "Tell me again, what happened on the Cypress Creek road?"

I recounted the incident.

"And the same man came to our house a few minutes ago?"

"It was the same creep," I insisted. "And Midnight actually liked him."

Mama smiled. "Maybe, just maybe, the man *wasn't* trying to threaten you on the Cypress Creek road."

"He was, too!" I snapped.

"Why would he come to our house to hurt you?"

"I don't know," I conceded. "I just know he rang our doorbell and," I showed Mama the oven spray can I was still clutching, "I was going to put his lights out for good."

"You might have blinded an innocent man."

"Yeah, right," I said, sarcastically.

"Simone, your father knows plenty of guys from all over Otis County. Some of them are his close buddies, others are acquaintances. This so-called 'creep,' as you call him, could have been coming to talk to James. Before we jump to any conclusions, let's ask James about this guy, okay?"

"That creep can't be one of Daddy's cronies," I protested.

"Young lady, the only thing you can get when you hurry is trouble. Let's wait and talk to your father. He'll help us get to the bottom of what that feller has on his mind."

"That man could very well be the same creep who was with Timber when Abe and Rick went chasing after him—"

Mama cut in. "We won't know until we've asked James, will we?" she asked, with a certain kind of emotion. I understood her tone. Despite the fact that at times my father drinks too much, Mama was convinced that he was quite capable of taking care of her and me.

I opened my mouth to argue with her. Reading my mind, she fastened her eyes on me. "James will find this young man, learn his intentions."

"You win," I said. "We'll wait until Daddy gets home." I looked down at the can of spray, then back into Mama's eyes. She smiled. I giggled. We both started laughing. Mama tried to stop laughing by putting her hand over her mouth, but she laughed again. I held up the can of oven spray and kept laughing. Tears streaked our faces and the laughter kept coming. I'd think I had gained control, then I'd look at Mama and be off again. I guess I didn't look like the fiercest protection Mama had ever had. Still laughing, I finally got up and put the can into the kitchen cupboard where it belonged.

We were eating lunch when Mama said, "At least that little incident this morning was worth a good laugh."

"I'd rather go to a comedy club," I said.

"You're not still upset?" she asked.

"No," I said, resignedly. "I admit it—I overreacted again."

Mama smiled. "You feel all right about taking me to see Abe?"

Her smile was contagious. "As long as I've got my oven cleaner handy," I joked.

"You sure you don't mind going into town?"

"I'm back to myself again. Besides, I think you're right. Daddy can handle that creep."

"I keep thinking," Mama said, "about how you said Midnight liked the young man."

"That crazy dog acted like he was a long-lost relative."

Mama looked concerned, but she didn't say any more about it.

Before we left the house, I made a phone call. "May I speak to Yasmine," I said, once I'd gotten the Atlanta number I'd dialed.

"Just a minute," a woman on the other end of the line said.

A few seconds later, Yasmine was on the phone. "Yasmine," I said.

"Simone, are you back in Atlanta?"

"No. I'm still in Otis."

Yasmine's voice dropped. "Oh."

"Listen, girlfriend," I said, trying to keep my voice controlled. "I've been thinking about our last talk and . . . well, to be honest, I don't believe either of us said all that we need to say to each other."

"Simone, you've decided *not* to go with me, haven't you?" she asked.

"I haven't made up my mind," I lied.

There was silence.

"I want you to come to Otis," I told Yasmine. "Come Sunday night, spend Monday here with me."

"What good will that do?"

"We could talk. I promise that before you leave, I will make a decision."

"You're not going with me."

"Three more days is all I'm asking," I told her. "Monday is your day off. Spend it with me here in Otis. After that, well—"

"You're not going to change your mind. I can tell from the sound of your voice, Simone."

"Please," I pleaded.

"Okay," Yasmine reluctantly agreed. "I'll come down on Sunday night."

I took a deep breath, then let it out loud enough for her to hear.

"Simone," she said, "you don't know what this thing is doing to me!"

"Hang in there," I told her, then said a quick good-bye and hung up. The truth is I still didn't know what I was going to say to Yasmine when she arrived in Otis. I only knew that we had to talk. We had to say things that would help our friendship through this crisis.

ELEVEN

The sheriff rubbed his eyes. He looked tired, like he'd missed a couple of nights' sleep. As usual, his office stank of cigarette smoke, but he didn't light up while we were there. "I've caught up with Joe Blake and Sonny Clay," he told Mama after she had been seated. "They both can account for themselves. But Les Demps left town the day after we found Cricket's body. It seems that Cricket had a thing going whereby she'd get these guys in some kind of situation that they didn't want people to know about. She'd somehow take their pictures. She guaranteed herself steady money by promising to keep the pictures to herself."

"I figured that," Mama said, with a nod. "I know a few other people in this town who're into that kind of thing. Fact is, though, if the men they mess with would stay away from them there wouldn't be any secrets to keep."

"Now, Candi," Abe said. "You and I both know that ain't likely to happen no time soon. Anyway," he continued, "I found out that Cricket and Les spent all day Monday in Savannah."

"And Clarence Young found Cricket's body in his apartment early Tuesday morning," Mama said.

Abe nodded.

"Did you check out Clarence's alibi?" Mama asked.

"I'm having trouble reaching the guy he was suppose to be working with. Right now, I ain't ruling Clarence Young out as a suspect either. By the way, Timber has been spotted again."

Mama leaned forward.

"He was in another car but with the same feller. They were on that stretch of road to Darien," Abe said. "A farmer called me, but by the time I got there, those two were long gone. Seems like that rascal is playing hide-and-seek with me."

"I think Timber is hanging around 'cause Morgan is still somewhere here in town," Mama said. "Rose told me that he was crazy about that child. And it might be that Timber didn't kill Cricket," Mama added.

"Then why won't he come in and talk to me?" Abe asked. "I done let it be known around the county that I'm not looking to arrest him, that I just want to talk to him about Cricket, that's all."

Mama shrugged. "He's probably scared."

"Can't be too scared," Abe insisted. "Seeing he don't mind being seen driving in and about the county in broad daylight."

"Abe," Mama said, "I'm thinking that Timber had another girlfriend. Somebody who might be keeping Morgan for him."

"I've talked to Timber's mother, Dollie Smith, about Timber's habits. Dollie told me that Timber was crazy about Cricket and little Morgan, that he wanted to marry Cricket but she'd have none of it. Dollie swears that Timber ain't never looked at another woman. Course Ellie Barker, the clerk at the hardware store, told me that Timber had somebody who was always giving him money. Said Timber bragged to her more than once that there was one person in Otis he could count on, and no matter what happened to him, that person would be there for him."

"Sounds like he was talking about his mama," I said, thinking that was exactly the way I felt about mine.

"I've talked to Steve Folks, the manager of Winn Dixie, and Mack Larson, the manager of Piggly Wiggly. They promised to have a meeting with their checkout clerks, tell them to be on the lookout for that baby. I also told them to watch to see if anybody comes in the store acting funny, you know, nervous."

"That's a good idea, Abe. Those clerks know everybody in town. But there's something stirring in my mind," Mama admitted. "Cricket's sister knows something that can help us, but she's confused. Or maybe scared, I'm not sure which."

"Rose never let anybody get too close," Abe replied.

Mama stood up. "Have you heard from the lab about the second skull Midnight brought home?"

Abe frowned. "Nothing yet," he said. His expression made me wonder whether he'd taken the time to send the second skull to the lab.

"I'm anxious to see that report," Mama told him. "And let me know when you talk to Les Demps. I'm going to stop by the hardware store and talk to Ellie Barker before Simone and I go back home."

"Don't look like we're any closer to finding that baby than we were a few days ago," Abe told Mama disappointedly.

"We're close," Mama said reassuringly. "We just don't know how close we are."

We stopped by the hardware store. Ellie Barker was on vacation; she wouldn't be back in town for a week.

Mama went into the family room when we got back home. She sat there for a long time, looking out into her garden. She had the same perplexed gaze. I glanced around, deciding that this was my favorite room in the house. The windows looking out into the garden, the comfortable furniture, the subtle shimmering of sunlight that fused the color of the room with the outdoors was almost magical.

Midnight was stretched out under his favorite tree in the backyard. For a second, he opened an eye, then he went back to sleep.

I hugged Mama. "What's on your mind, pretty lady?" I asked.

"So many things," she replied, with a slight sigh.

"Would a cup of coffee help?"

"Vanilla chocolate," she said promptly. But she kept staring thoughtfully out into the garden, her look troubled.

When the coffee was ready, I poured Mama a cup. Finally, in an effort to get her to become more talkative, I said, "If we can find that creep who came here this morning, we'll find Morgan Childs!"

"If 'the creep,' as you keep calling him, Simone, knows anything about that poor child, James will find out. But I don't think it's that simple."

Her voice was a little stern. I knew now that she was adamant that the man I was so sure was a villain was simply a misunderstood soul who had mistakenly frightened me.

I poured myself a cup of coffee and decided that sometimes Mama could be wrong in her judgment of people. That guy in the blue Ford was a villain, no matter what Mama—and Midnight—might think of him.

"I can't stop thinking about that little cemetery in the back of Rose's trailer," Mama said.

"We know Cricket's grandmother, Miss Lucy Bell Childs, started the graves."

"I got a hunch. Let's go, Simone."

"Where are we heading?" I asked.

"To the community center," Mama answered. "That's where we'll find *my* 'sources,' this time of day."

The Otis Community Center is on Oak Street. A lot of community activities take place there, but every afternoon between three and four, senior citizens get together and sew, or work some kind of arts and crafts.

"This is where we can find Sarah, Annie Mae, and Carrie this time of day," Mama told me, stepping into the center.

The big room was filled with folding tables. About twenty gray-headed women were sitting on folding chairs, working with brightly colored swatches of cloth. The smell of lavender air freshener hung heavy in the air.

"They're working on a community quilt," Mama told me, looking around until she spotted Sarah, Carrie, and Annie Mae sitting in the far corner of the room. They were so busy talking, they were barely touching the pieces of cloth in their hands.

I followed Mama to where they were seated. The three women were surprised to see us. "My Lord, Candi!" Sarah exclaimed. "What are you doing strutting around on those feet like a teenager?

You ain't got no business out and about for at least six weeks."

Mama smiled. "I'm doing okay," she said. "But you're right, Sarah, I'm going to take it easy."

"What you doing here?" Carrie asked. "You ain't here to help us with the quilt, are you?"

"No," Mama replied. "I'm here because I want to ask you ladies a question."

All three women folded their hands in their laps, sat back in their chairs, and looked as if they were ready and willing to dispense any information Mama needed.

"Lucy Bell Childs," Mama began. "Is she still living?"

Sarah laughed. "That old woman died twenty years ago."

Mama's eyes twinkled.

"Lucy Bell was the county's only midwife. She worked with old Dr. Fields," Annie Mae volunteered.

"Problem was, Miss Lucy Bell didn't cotton to her special calling," Carrie Smalls said.

I didn't understand. "Calling?" I asked.

Mama chuckled. "Being a midwife was considered a calling back then, Simone. It was special, like being a preacher."

"Trouble was," Sarah Jenkins said, "Lucy Bell didn't like delivering babies. She scorned the women whenever they called on her. She didn't keep her feelings to herself either. While the women were having their babies, they would be hearing Lucy Bell's sermon against getting pregnant in the first place. Added to that, after Lucy Bell delivered the baby, she'd threaten to strangle it."

"You're kidding!" I exclaimed, horrified.

Annie Mae Gregory took up the report. "The women of Otis County were willing to put up with Lucy Bell's insolence until the latter part of 1970. That's when the babies Lucy Bell delivered began contracting a fever a few days after they were born. Those poor children didn't live long after that. From birth to death was about six months for each child."

Sarah Jenkins continued the story. "Lucy Bell delivered an infant to Nadie Wright. Nadie already had ten children, so when Nadie's baby caught the fever, she couldn't take care of it. Somebody told her that since she'd endured Lucy's wrath during her delivery, and since Lucy Bell had threatened harm to the child, Lucy Bell was to blame for the child's sickness. Somehow, Nadie talked Lucy Bell into taking that sick child to care for it until it recovered. After Nadie left her baby, every other baby that Lucy Bell delivered who contracted the fever ended up in Lucy Bell's care."

"The children all died?" I asked.

The three women nodded.

"Why the graveyard?" Mama asked.

Carrie Smalls answered. "I suppose Lucy Bell thought it right to bury the poor little things herself right there in the field behind her house rather than take their bodies back to their parents."

"After a while," Annie Mae told us, "the women stopped calling Lucy Bell when they got in labor.

They crossed the county line and got another midwife."

"And the fever?" Mama asked.

"It stopped," Sarah replied.

"So, Lucy Bell Childs was the carrier?" Mama asked.

"That's what people say," Carrie said, shaking her head sorrowfully.

I felt a pinch of sorrow, thinking of those twelve gravestones in the grass behind Rose Childs's trailer.

Forty-five minutes later, when we were sitting in our garden, Mama said to me, "Knowing the good folks here in Otis, they probably stopped fooling with Lucy Bell altogether. I imagined the poor woman spent many nights alone, sitting, holding a sick baby."

"She probably grew to love those babies," I said.

"It's hard to imagine taking care of an infant, sick or well, and not getting attached to it," Mama said.

"Her love for the babies must be what I felt in that cemetery."

"What?" Mama asked.

"When I was standing in Lucy Bell's cemetery, I got a funny feeling. It was something more than just being among the dead."

Her face brightened. " 'The way to love anything is to realize that it might be lost,' " she quoted.

"What?"

The look in Mama's eyes told me that something had just clicked. She nodded, like she'd just made an important decision. "Simone, first thing tomorrow

morning I want you to go out to Lucy Bell's cemetery. I want you to carefully take a picture of each
headstone."

"Rose will kill me." I balked, remembering Rose
and the fierce way she protected her family secrets.

Mama gestured me into the house. She picked up
the phone and dialed a number. "Rose," she began.
Her voice was gentle but there was no mistaking its
air of command. "This is Candi. How are you today? . . . Listen, I have a little money I'd like to
give you to help with Cricket's burial expenses. . . .
I meant to give it to you the other day when I
visited. . . . Do me a favor, and stop by in the morning . . . around nine is fine . . . Give me a few minutes
to get to the door, it's not easy walking on stitched-
up feet. . . . Okay, I'll see you tomorrow morning
around nine o'clock." She put the phone back on its
receiver.

I stood beside her, still not impressed. "Mama,
Cricket's whole family lives on that land," I protested.
"The place is like a commune. If I go there snooping
around with a camera, somebody is bound to see me
and feel obliged to shoot me for trespassing."

"If anybody questions what you're doing, just tell
them that Rose gave you permission to take the
pictures."

"That wouldn't be true," I pointed out.

Mama raised an eyebrow, exasperated. "Simone,
little Morgan's life is on the line. We've got to find
that child."

I recalled the beguiling eyes of the beautiful baby,

the eyes that had so captivated me and changed my feelings about children and becoming a mother.

"Don't worry," Mama reassured me. "I'll fix it with Rose. I need to look at the names on those headstones."

"Then I'll take the pictures while you entertain Rose," I agreed, frowning at Mama, but still thinking of Morgan. "I just hope your need to see those names don't cause you to end up attending my funeral," I muttered drily.

A flicker of a smile touched Mama's lips—she thought I was overreacting again. Then, abruptly, her look changed. I followed her gaze. She was staring at Midnight. In the yard outside the window, the dog had sat up and yawned.

"What are you trying to tell me, Midnight?" Mama murmured. "*What do you want me to do about those babies' skulls you've dug up and brought home to James?*"

TWELVE

Mama's face lights up whenever one of my brothers calls. Today was no different. My youngest brother, Will, phoned from Orlando. No sooner had she put the phone back on its receiver than Rodney called from New York.

Minutes after that, Daddy phoned to say that he had to work late; he wouldn't be home until after six. Around three, the florist delivered roses from both my brothers.

After the flowers were arranged in vases, Mama said, "Simone, let me tell you how to make a lasagna." Once it was pulled together and inside the oven, I joined Mama in the family room. She was stretched out on the sofa, her feet propped up on three pillows.

"Yasmine is coming on Sunday evening," I told her, trying to sound casual.

Mama's eyebrow rose.

"I've asked her to stay until Monday afternoon."

"I suggest you cook something simple, like baked chicken. What we don't eat Sunday, we can have for Monday's lunch. And there are blanched vegetables in the freezer. It'll be easy to prepare a nice casserole."

I shuddered. By now the aroma of my lasagna was beginning to tantalize, but that same scent poignantly reminded me of how much I missed Mama's cooking.

To my relief, Mama didn't ask why I'd invited Yasmine. But she had a look that told me she suspected something: I guess she was so busy with her own mysteries that she decided to let what was going on between me and Yasmine slip past.

When Daddy came home that night, Mama didn't broach the subject of the creep's visit until well after he'd eaten his supper. He was sitting in his favorite chair, drinking a beer. "James, a young man came by the house today," she began nonchalantly.

Daddy swallowed deeply from his bottle.

"Simone, tell your father about the young man."

I started describing the creep and how threatening he looked when my father broke out into a loud laugh. "Simone, baby, you're talking about Nightmare."

Mama sat straight up. "James, what's the boy's *real* name?" she asked.

"I don't know, baby," he answered. "People have

been calling that boy Nightmare all his life. I reckon only his mama knows Nightmare's given name."

"Who are his people?" Mama asked.

"His mama was a Givens. His daddy's name was Leman Childs."

Mama's eyes widened. "That boy is kin to Cricket Childs?"

Daddy took another draught from his beer. "Nightmare and Cricket are first cousins, brothers' children."

"I was right," I said, excited. "I did see Morgan in the backseat of Nightmare's car!"

Mama held up a hand to quiet me. "Wait a minute, Simone," she said. "Why would that boy come *here*?"

Daddy's eyes were still laughing. " 'Cause I asked him to."

"You did *what*?"

"Nightmare is the best hunter around," Daddy answered. "When he's not trying to scare people, he catches all kinds of wild game. I saw him in town this morning and told him to bring me a slab of that venison he said he had in his freezer."

I felt an uneasiness, a sense that something was wrong with what I'd just heard. "Mama," I said, "Rose was lying to us—*Nightmare* is hiding Morgan."

Mama took a deep breath. "I guess you were right about him," she said.

"He's got Morgan," I repeated, "and when he saw me, he tried to hurt me."

Daddy looked confused. "What did Nightmare try to do to you?"

I told him about the incident on the Cypress

Creek road. Daddy leaned back and shook his head. "Simone, baby, Nightmare looks spooky, but he's harmless."

"He tried to grab me but—"

Daddy interrupted. "You're not the first woman Nightmare has pulled that trick on, Simone. That's probably how he got his nickname. Fact is, that boy gets his kicks from trying to scare women. He especially likes that road because it's a long stretch and seldom used. But he's never hurt a soul."

I swore. "That creep!"

Daddy grinned at the irritation in my voice. "Abe's always warning him about doing that. He's even threatened to lock him up, but it hasn't stopped Nightmare."

"Suppose I had a weak heart? He could have scared me to death," I retorted hotly.

"Worse still," Mama said, "Simone could have blinded him with that can of oven cleaner she found in the cabinet."

Daddy looked surprised. "What about the oven cleaner?" he asked in a flat, hard voice.

"Next time, I'll be *his* nightmare," I vowed.

"What about this oven cleaner?" Daddy repeated.

I refused to answer so Mama had to tell him about how I was prepared to open the front door and greet Nightmare. "You'd better let that boy know how close he came to harm, James," she cautioned. "Maybe if you can get him to understand how his antics might provoke somebody into hurting him, he'll stop his foolishness."

Daddy didn't say anything. Instead, he nodded, his expression one of concern.

"Tell him that I resent his tricks and that he's messing with the wrong black woman." I was still angry.

Mama frowned. "Those were Cricket's exact words," she murmured.

"What?" I asked.

"I was thinking that Cricket told Birdie those same words. In Winn Dixie last Saturday."

"Oh, yeah." Only six days had passed but so much had happened since that incident. The anger in Cricket's eyes when she hollered at Birdie flashed through my mind. And now she was dead and crazy Nightmare had her baby.

"Poor Morgan." Mama shook her head. "There must be a reason that her family is hiding that baby and letting everybody in the county believe that the child has been kidnapped!"

"Maybe the whole family are a bunch of nuts," I retorted.

Daddy's frown was so deep, his nose wrinkled. "Nightmare is a little off. But the rest of the family have good sense."

Mama studied Daddy carefully, as if she was trying to put her finger on something he might know but that he wasn't clear about. "James, have you had much conversation with Nightmare?"

"We've talked from time to time," Daddy said. "Why?"

"I was wondering whether he's ever mentioned his grandmother, Lucy Bell Childs."

"Can't say I remember anything about his grandmother."

"What about Cricket?" I asked.

"No, he ain't never mentioned Cricket either."

There was a brief silence. "Has Nightmare ever mentioned the cemetery behind Rose's trailer?" Mama prompted.

Daddy made a dismissive gesture with his hand. "No. I never knew there was a cemetery."

Mama shook her head. "Simone, tomorrow morning when you take those pictures, Rose will be here with me, and this time she *is* going to tell me what's behind all this secrecy!"

It was dawn, Saturday morning. I was awakened from a sound sleep by Midnight's deep-throated woof and my father's voice. I enjoy waking up to the fragrance of summer flowers and the chirping of sparrows in Mama's yard. But this morning, instead of being gently prodded to get out of my bed, I was snatched up by the serious argument going on in our backyard between my father and his best friend.

Even though my mind wasn't clear, I knew that what was going down had to do with Midnight's not wanting to be tied up.

"Boy," my father was saying, "you can't keep bringing home things that don't belong to us."

I couldn't tell by his frantic barks whether Midnight understood my father's reasoning or not.

I yawned.

Midnight's yelps grew louder. "Quiet down, boy," I heard Daddy say. "You're going to wake Candi and she needs her rest."

Then my father said, "I want you back in this yard in an hour, you hear?"

Midnight stopped barking; there wasn't even a small whimper. I wondered whether he understood his curfew.

I headed to the kitchen toward the rich smell of French vanilla coffee.

"Sounds like you and Midnight had a fight," I said when Daddy came inside.

Daddy's expression was sour. "Yeah," he admitted, then poured himself a cup of coffee and sat down.

I walked behind his chair and put my hands on his shoulders and began rubbing them. "Sounds like you lost."

Daddy's smile was a thin grin of embarrassment. "It's not Midnight's style to be tied to a tree."

"I can believe that," I said. I poured myself a cup of coffee, then joined my father.

Daddy frowned. "Baby, your mama's right— The thing to do is not to chain Midnight but to find where he's been digging. Folks in this town don't cater to desecrating their dead."

I lifted my cup and breathed in the wonderful scent of the coffee. "Did Mama tell you that Abe is expecting a report from SLED's lab on Monday?"

Daddy sipped his coffee. "Yeah," he said. "I sure

wish Midnight would go back to dragging home things that I can pay for, like boots from back porches. There's something unholy about disturbing the dead."

"Especially dead babies," I whispered, thinking about Morgan Childs.

THIRTEEN

The sun was bright. Swarms of mosquitoes, like tiny black snowflakes, floated in the humid air.

As I had done the day before, I parked my Honda behind Rose Childs's trailer. Then I waited for somebody else in the family to come out and throw me off their property.

Instead, all was quiet. Too quiet. Mama's plan to draw Rose away from the cemetery by getting her to come over to our house for money to help with the funeral expenses was clever. Except that Rose lived on what I considered the Childses' commune. Lots more family would be around to hinder me from taking pictures. On my drive here, I'd decided to deal with their resistance up front, before I was down on my hands and knees taking snapshots of the tiny, old graves.

Now, however, there wasn't a stir from any of the mobile homes. Only the smell of green peppers and onions cooking.

There wasn't a sound, not even a barking dog or a television set.

I stood for a moment gazing down the road at the rows of neat mobile homes, swatting mosquitoes away from my face. Then I walked over, unlatched the gate, and stepped inside the graveyard.

Out of a natural reverence for the dead, I stopped for a moment. I studied the well-groomed graveyard, the little headstones. The only sign of life was a brown spider scurrying over the headstone of Eyelet Combs, born June 1, 1969, died December 25, 1969.

I stood there, imagining Miss Lucy Bell Childs holding tiny Eyelet, who would have been wrapped in some sort of handmade clothes. Lucy Bell probably sewed something special for Eyelet's final moments aboveground. I wondered how Eyelet looked, what uniqueness she had brought into the world. Then the thought of how short and tragic the lives of all twelve of these babies were made me shiver in sadness.

Miss Lucy Bell's helplessness as she nursed poor, dying Eyelet and each of the other eleven infants while watching their lives slip away must have been overwhelming. I remembered Annie Mae Gregory's remark that Miss Lucy Bell hated being called a midwife.

As I stood thinking, I saw in my mind's eye an old

woman in a black dress that draped her from neck to ankles. Her snow-colored kinky hair would have been covered with a large white handkerchief, a custom of women in this area whenever they didn't want to wear a hat to church. Her shoes would have been black, polished to a high gleam.

Her scent would have been of lavender extract. Miss Lucy Bell would have given each dead child its last bath in spiced water so as to present it as a sweet-smelling odor to its Maker.

I imagined her standing with tiny, lifeless Eyelet Combs in her arms. Lucy would quote a scripture, sing a song, pray.

I imagined the deep sadness in her face. A surge of compassion swept through me. To Miss Lucy Bell, this pretty, quiet place was more than a cemetery; it was a shrine of her atonement for begrudging her mission of bringing these poor babies into the world. And perhaps for being the carrier of some germ that had cut their young lives so short.

Something moved. I looked toward the trees. Nothing. "Oh, well," I said to myself, "Mama sent me to take pictures. I'd better hop to it." I swatted another mosquito on my neck, then pulled Mama's Olympus camera from its case.

It must have been a half hour later when I became aware of the sound of blowflies and the smell of fresh-killed flesh. This new, unpleasant scent came from the woods. Barely visible at the edge of the trees, I saw a figure. A large, hulking man with a straggly beard.

And then, without warning, he was gone. For a second, I wasn't quite sure I'd seen him at all. But I knew who it was.

Nightmare was trying to scare me, getting his kicks again by provoking the same kind of fear in me that he'd aroused when I was driving to Cousin Agatha's house. But this time I wasn't going to be intimidated by some half-witted boogeyman.

I was crouched, shooting angles of the final resting place of an infant who had died just three days before the death of Eyelet Combs. The name on the tombstone was Tony Tabard, born July 1, died December 22. Then I heard rustling in a nearby bush. I stood. But there was no sign of the hulking man who seemed to be shadowing me. I decided the sound I'd heard was just some small creature foraging in the underbrush. So I jumped and nearly dropped Mama's camera when Nightmare said, very close to me: "What you doing in Grandma Lucy Bell's graveyard? Who are you?"

Even though I'd expected him to show up, I froze. I scanned the landscape as if I was searching for a place to hide. The seconds stretched out. My fingers tightened on Mama's camera. Then I took a deep breath, filling my nostrils with Nightmare's tangy scent, one of fresh blood and sweat.

"I said, what you doing messing with some of Grandma Lucy Bell's babies?" he repeated impatiently.

I stood up and turned to face him. "It doesn't matter who *I* am. I know who *you* are."

I was staring Nightmare square in the face. He did indeed look like somebody who'd been conjured up in a bad dream. He sneered, then moved toward me. A cynical grin twisted his lips. In his right hand was a knife, in his left the carcass of a fat rabbit whose abdomen had been slit. The dead animal dripped blood on Nightmare's filthy boots.

A gust of warm air stirred and a swarm of flies rose around him and his odor. I swallowed the lump in my throat, determined to speak a lot more confidently than I felt. "Just who do you think you are?" I demanded. "And where do you get off scaring women? Don't you know that you could make a person hurt you or themselves when all you're doing is having some stupid kind of fun?"

Nightmare stared at me with flat brown eyes. Then he wiped his brow with his right hand, the hand with the knife. "I done ask you once, what you doing messing with Grandma Lucy Bell's babies?" But his voice had moderated a little, as if he'd sensed my determination not to be frightened off.

"I'm not doing anything that would interest you," I snapped. I took a step toward the open gate.

Nightmare's dark eyes instantly filled with suspicion. He moved toward me. "Nobody suppose to be messing with these babies," he said.

I decided not to say anything. I'd just wait until he grabbed for me, then I'd give him a good jab directly into his stupid eyes. But then I had an idea. "Listen, you creep, I'm James Covington's daughter," I said.

Nightmare stopped cold. He stared as if making

up his mind whether I was telling him the truth. Then, lowering his knife, he stepped back. "Mr. James sent you for his venison, didn't he?" he asked.

"No, he did not," I answered.

He wiped his nose, then offered me the carcass. "He sent you for one of my rabbits?"

"No. My father didn't send me for anything." I put my hands on my hips. "Listen, you tried to scare me on the road to Cypress Creek the other day and I want you to know that I didn't appreciate it. If you do that to me again, I'll ram my tire jack down your throat."

A flicker of satisfaction crossed Nightmare's ugly face. "You're scared now, ain't you?" he asked.

"Hell, no!" I snapped, shaking my head. I turned and strolled out of the cemetery. Behind me, Nightmare laughed. "This creep is really crazy," I muttered under my breath. But I kept walking.

Through his laughter, Nightmare called out: "Mr. James's gal, you're scared right now. You can't fool Nightmare, you're scared right now!"

I turned to face him, holding Mama's camera tight. "If you ever try that again," I warned, sickened at the pleasure in his eyes, "what I leave as your face in one piece, my father will cut up like that rabbit, do you hear me, creep?"

Nightmare's grin widened. He gestured with his left hand, the dead rabbit dangling in midair. "Nightmare can tell you be real scared right now," he said smugly.

By this time I'd gotten to my Honda, had opened the door, and was sitting behind the wheel. I tossed Mama's camera on the passenger's seat and switched on the ignition.

Nightmare's crazy laughter ricocheted through the still hot air. "Mr. James won't do nothing to hurt Nightmare," he shouted confidently. "Mr. James *likes* Nightmare's venison!"

CHAPTER

FOURTEEN

It was a little after eleven o'clock when I finally got the film to the drugstore. I asked for their one-hour developing. When I got back to the house, Mama was stretched out on the sofa. Rose Childs sat in an easy chair nearby. I said hello, then headed straight toward the kitchen to get a cold drink.

"Sometimes, Rose," I heard Mama say, "keeping things to yourself is the best thing to do."

When Rose answered, her voice was low and tense like she didn't want anybody to hear. "I don't like people getting into my business."

"I can understand how you feel," Mama agreed. She sounded relaxed, gracious.

"People always looking to say something bad,

always trying to find fault." Rose paused. "Lord knows, I did what I thought was right."

"Nobody can blame you for anything," Mama said.

I walked into the family room, tilting a glass of Coke up to my lips. "Simone," Mama said curtly, "I'm surprised you didn't offer Rose or me a cold drink."

I shrugged, turned, and headed back for the refrigerator. A few minutes later, I handed both Rose and Mama a glass of cola.

"Still, Rose," Mama was saying, "there are times when a burden becomes too heavy to bear alone. That's when you need to talk with somebody you can trust."

Rose stopped the glass halfway to her lips. She gave Mama a quick, suspicious glance.

"There are people who know how to keep a confidence," Mama told her.

Rose looked down into her glass.

"There's something heavy on your mind, isn't there, Rose?" Mama asked.

Rose looked into Mama's eyes, her lips twitching.

Mama said, "I believe it's got something to do with poor Cricket's murder."

Rose blinked. "I don't want people saying bad things about me."

"I can't imagine anybody thinking bad of you," Mama told her. "But if what you've got on your mind is something you want me and Simone to keep to ourselves, I can understand that."

Rose nodded but still she said nothing.

Mama eased back against the sofa cushions. "As long as what's bothering you doesn't have anything to do with breaking the law or hindering Abe from catching up with Cricket's killer, I see no reason for me or Simone to repeat it. Your secret is our secret, isn't that right, Simone?" Mama asked me.

I nodded, placed my empty glass on the table, sat in the chair next to Rose, and waited.

For a while, Rose didn't speak. She sat, biting her lip and rubbing her half-empty glass with her fingertips. Finally, she said, "I reckoned I should have paid more attention—" She stopped.

"To what?" Mama asked gently.

Rose let out a breath that sounded like a sorrowful sigh. "To what Cricket said about somebody wanting to take little Morgan."

"Go on," Mama said.

"Six weeks ago, Cricket found a note on her car windshield," Rose continued. "It said, *Morgan is pretty enough to steal.*"

"Sounds like a compliment to me. That child is real pretty."

"Cricket thought so, too. Then a week later she found another note. This one read, *Tainted blood runs inside you.*"

Mama frowned.

Rose continued. "Cricket asked me what to do. I told her not to put too much stock in it."

"What happened to the notes?" I asked.

"I guess she threw them away," Rose answered.

"There was another note, wasn't there?" Mama asked.

Rose nodded, looking miserable. "The third note read, *Morgan suppose to be mine.*"

I thought Mama was going to say something, but to my surprise she was silent. Rose took a stuttering breath. "It pains me that Cricket was going to take that note to the sheriff but I talked her out of it."

"For heaven's sake, why?" I demanded. If Abe had known about those threats, maybe Cricket would be alive today.

"I told her Timber wrote the notes. He had strong feelings for Morgan, and he hated that Cricket was working with Sabrina Miley. He's jumped on Cricket to fight her more than once because he hated that Sabrina was taking money from men because she knew things that they wanted to keep secret. For the past few months, Timber has even been threatening to have the welfare take Morgan away from Cricket, but Cricket told him that she wasn't scared of that— that the people at the welfare knew how much she loved Morgan and what good care she gave that child."

"And when Birdie snatched Morgan out of Cricket's car?" I asked. "That day at the Winn Dixie?"

"Cricket went ballistic on Birdie when she caught up with her. But she still believed that Timber was behind those notes." Rose sighed. "Everybody knows that Birdie has a nerve problem and as long as she takes her medicine, she's okay. But, whenever she misses a few doses, she gets confused."

Mama spoke. "Abe told me that he's had a good talk with Isaiah, Birdie's husband. Isaiah has promised to make sure that Birdie takes her medicine." She turned to look at me. "Simone, you saw her on Wednesday fishing with Koot. She seemed okay, don't you think?"

I nodded.

Rose rolled her eyes. "Timber . . ." Rose stopped, and started again. "I expect I should tell Abe that Timber wrote those notes and that he killed Cricket so that him and *some* woman could take the child."

Mama looked confused. "I don't follow you."

Rose cocked her head and frowned. "Last Monday morning," she said, "Timber came and told Cricket that he wanted to take Morgan to visit his mama. At first Cricket said no, but then she remembered she wanted to go off to Savannah with one of her men. And Timber swore that his mama had clothes and money for the child and she only wanted to keep the baby for a few hours. So, Cricket finally said okay. But when she got back home around nine o'clock that night and discovered that Timber hadn't brought Morgan back, she called his mama's house. Timber's mama told Cricket that she hadn't seen Timber or Morgan in weeks. Cricket called the sheriff but when she couldn't reach him, she headed out to hunt for Timber herself."

"Did you talk to Cricket after that?" I asked.

Rose's voice rose. "No. The next day, Abe and that deputy of his, Rick Martin, came and told me that Cricket had been killed."

"And Morgan?" Mama asked. "Have you seen Morgan since Cricket died?"

Rose said very softly, like she was in great misery, "I've talked to Timber's mama. She swears that not she, nor anybody else in her family, knows Morgan's whereabouts."

I held my hands up. "Wait a minute," I protested. "I happen to know for a fact that somebody in *your* family is hiding Morgan."

Rose looked at me, surprised.

"Daddy told me that big ugly guy who folks call Nightmare is your cousin, isn't that right?" I asked, scowling at the memory of the big stinking man holding up his dead rabbit and laughing tauntingly at me.

Rose nodded.

"The same Nightmare who gets his kicks from scaring women."

"He's a little touched in the head," Rose conceded, "but he doesn't mean no harm."

"Touched in the head or not, his little tricks could get him hurt," I continued. "Especially if he tries to pull another one on me."

"When did you see Nightmare?" Rose asked.

"On Tuesday afternoon," I said, "I saw Morgan in Nightmare's blue sedan." I wasn't about to tell Rose about my encounter with Nightmare a few hours ago in her grandmother's graveyard.

Rose leaned back in her chair and knitted her hands together. "You didn't see Morgan."

"On Tuesday afternoon, the day after Cricket was murdered, I was driving on the Cypress Creek road going to Cousin Agatha's. I saw Morgan in her car seat in the back of Nightmare's car. I'll swear to that!"

Rose's shoulders relaxed; her look softened a little. She put down her glass. "You saw my daughter Trice's baby, Lizzie, with Nightmare," she told me. "He was bringing her back from Miss Lottie's house."

"I saw Morgan," I said.

"I'll tell you what you saw," Rose said. "Lizzie was born a week before Morgan was born. Lizzie's daddy is Bo, Miss Lottie Bing's youngest son. Since both Trice and Bo are in their last year of school, Miss Lottie keeps Lizzie during the day. I get Lizzie ready before I go to work and Nightmare takes her to Miss Lottie every morning. In the afternoon, he picks Lizzie up and brings her home."

I stood and walked toward the window. "I could have sworn that was Morgan I saw," I insisted.

Mama glanced at me, then at Rose. "Let's get back to Timber's mama," she said. "You sound like you don't believe her when she says that they aren't hiding Morgan."

Rose looked away, out of the window toward the garden. For a moment, she didn't speak. Then she said, "I don't mean no disrespect, Miss Candi, but everybody know that all of Timber's people are natural-born liars."

There had been ominous portents of an approaching storm all day. The air was turbulent, erratic, humid. The sky was charcoal instead of blue. A hot breeze sent leaves scuttling along the highway.

The women's voices swelled above the claps of thunder. I looked out of the window of the cinderblock building. Lightning struck near the parking lot, briefly illuminating the sky. A crash of thunder followed. Moments later, the rain came, pouring from the dark sky like an avalanche.

It was Saturday afternoon, four o'clock. Inside the Baptist church, the hot air smelled of flowers and dampness.

Mourners filled the church, men dressed in dark suits, women in black dresses. They'd come to say good-bye to Cricket Childs. There were a number of people I didn't know, but most of them were sitting with people I did. Some were Cricket's relatives. Others were people Mama had talked to me about, people she'd told me stories of.

My mother was dressed in a navy blue silk dress. I wore a black suit that I always kept in Mama's closet cleaned and readied for these occasions. We were sitting in the fifth row, almost at the back of the church. We had no problem hearing the choir's song; the singers were determined not to let the torrent outside drown out their voices.

I glanced at Mama. She was leaning forward, a look on her face that I can only describe as watchful; she looked like a good boxer studying his opponent.

Another clap of thunder seemed to shake the little building. The frowns on the faces of those gathered in the church told me that I wasn't the only one who was wondering how hard it was going to be to get to Rose's home after the funeral.

The preacher stood up, his pulpit high above Cricket's bronze-colored coffin, which sat on a stand in front of it. He was a bowed little man with woolly gray hair and a flat nose. But his black eyes were piercing. He stood silently for a moment, making eye contact with everybody who looked at him. Then he opened his Bible and read a scripture. He had a low voice, almost lost in the sound of the storm overhead. I expected him to speak louder, like his choir, but he didn't do it. It was like he was too tired to compete with what was plunging from the sky.

After his sermon, three people spoke about Cricket's family. All testified to the Childses' character, their place in the community.

Finally the preacher stood up again and said, "Let us pray." All heads bowed. I nudged Mama and whispered, "Let's get out of here before the crowd."

Mama nodded. "When they stand to view Cricket's body, we'll leave," she told me.

A few minutes later, we had to ease past two morticians who stood, like bodyguards, at the church's open doors.

We were out of the church and on its steps when Mama stopped abruptly. She looked down on the parked cars. The rain hammered down. She shook her head, frowning. "That's strange," she murmured.

"Stay here," I urged. "I'll bring the car to you." Then I dashed through the rain to my Honda.

The rain was steady, slicing through my headlights, the wipers barely able to keep up. A bolt of lightning cut through the sky. "Simone,"—Mama was straining to see through the storm—"watch out for that station wagon!"

"I see it," I said.

She took a deep breath. "Did you see who was driving?" she asked, watching through the back window as the speeding car faded from sight.

My hands gripped the steering wheel. My eyes were glued to the road in front of me. "I saw a woman with a hat."

Rain swept across the road; wind shook the car.

"I thought—" Mama began, then paused. "Could I have been wrong both times?" she murmured. Half of my mind was listening. The other half was thinking what a horrible day it was to be buried.

"You missed the turnoff," Mama said.

"I'll turn around soon as I can," I told her.

When I finally got to the right road, the Childses' mobile-home commune popped up in my headlights like an oasis. The rain began tapering off; the thunderhead, still spitting jagged bolts of lightning, was moving north.

I drove slowly to Rose's trailer, parked, and turned off the headlights. Mama reached into the backseat and picked up her gray plastic raincoat.

A pretty young girl, about sixteen, with gleaming dark eyes, opened Rose's door and ushered us into a screened wooden porch. In the girl's arms was a baby about the same age as Morgan, a child that I could have indeed mistaken for Morgan. The baby, who I suspected was named Lizzie, made a noise, something that sounded like a hiccup. "Shhh," the girl with the beautiful dark eyes whispered gently to the infant.

We stepped inside out of the drizzle. The girl reached behind her with her free hand, then handed Mama a clean towel.

The sleepy eyes of young Lizzie were in stark contrast to those of the other children who came out from a room in the back of the mobile home to stare at us.

"Go back into that bedroom!" the girl hollered at them. They darted back inside.

We rubbed our arms dry with the towels, then the girl ushered us inside a large bright room. For some reason, I didn't remember seeing the two walls of books with faded bindings when Mama and I had visited Rose earlier. They must have caught Mama's eyes, too, because she studied them thoughtfully.

But I did remember the framed pictures of young boys and girls on the mantel. Today, however, there was another photo, a black-and-white picture of an old woman.

The room smelled of food, that delicious blend of aromas that's unique to Southern postfuneral visits with grieving families. Neighbors and relatives had carted food in for the feast. A long wooden table draped in a brand-new white plastic tablecloth ran the width of the room. On it were at least five different kinds of potato salad. There were candied sweet potatoes, carrot shuffle, white rice, collard greens, string beans, and new potatoes spiced with smoked sausages. There was succotash, carrot and raisin salads, lima beans, okra fritters, macaroni and cheese, lasagna, black beans and rice, red rice, corn bread, biscuits, fried chicken, ham, turkey stuffed with a corn bread dressing, meat loaf, Swedish meatballs in tomato sauce, baked beans, bread pudding with a poignant whisky sauce, pound cakes, sweet potatoes, apple pies, and mountains of cookies. The display seemed overwhelming. Mama's contribution, a carrot-sweet potato puree, sat in the center of the table on a large crystal platter garnished with sprigs of mint. Mama had confided that she'd prepared for this kind of event before she had her surgery. Stashed away in her freezer were several very special dishes, among them this puree.

Mama had told me its ingredients when she asked me to pull it from the freezer: sour cream, whipping cream, sweet potatoes, carrots, salt, sugar, butter, nutmeg, black pepper, red pepper, and margarine. She'd instructed me to let it thaw overnight in the refrigerator. And before we left to go to Cricket's funeral, I'd baked the puree for thirty minutes. My father, not one for attending funerals unless it was a family member, had offered to drop it off at Rose's mobile home while we were in church.

I surveyed the rest of the room. Behind the table was the couch and three or four matching cushioned chairs. At least a dozen gray plastic folding chairs lined the walls, left, no doubt, by the undertaker for guests.

Mama sat down in one of the cushioned chairs; I flopped on the couch. "Honey," Mama asked the young woman who'd let us in, "what's your name?"

Dimples formed in the girl's cheeks as she flashed a smile at Mama. "My name is Trice."

"Are you Rose's daughter?" I asked.

Trice nodded. "I'm her oldest daughter," she said, looking over her shoulder. Then, in a sharp voice, she yelled down the hall to the clustered, staring children, "Get back in that bedroom and shut the door!"

Mama studied the photograph of the old lady with an intensity that was almost embarrassing. She pointed. "Trice, tell me—who is that?"

Trice made a slight movement of her head, almost a nod, then she cocked her head in the picture's direction. "That's Great-grandma Lucy Bell," she answered.

I stirred in my seat. "I don't remember seeing that picture before," I said.

"It was put out this morning," she told me. Again impatience flashed on her face as she turned to see that the five or six children were almost inside the living room with us. She patted her sleeping baby on the back, turned, and walked toward the children. "I done told all of you, you've got to stay inside the bedroom while Mama's company is here, do you hear me?"

At that moment, the door banged open and a crowd of people pushed inside the room. All the chairs quickly became filled. Fingers started tasting from the food on the table. I was going to suggest to Mama that I fix a plate for both of us when Rose, dressed all in black, stepped between us. She bent and whispered something in Mama's ear, something that caused Mama to blink in confusion. Whatever Mama responded, it caused Rose to shake her head emphatically.

Mama patted Rose on the hands. I heard her say, "Tonight, no matter how late, I'll expect you."

Rose nodded, broke off eye contact, and moved back quietly to the other side of the room.

"What's that all about?" I asked, once I'd gotten close enough to whisper in Mama's ear.

"Rose has found something that Lucy Bell had kept hidden all these years!" Mama told me.

CHAPTER

SIXTEEN

I finished my coffee and looked at my watch: 10:06. I took a deep breath, walked to the glass door, and looked out into the garden.

Just a few drops of rain had fallen on the windshield as we'd driven home from Rose's house. Now the southern sky was crystal clear. There wasn't one cloud overhead. The stars sent their lights in all directions.

Mama took her last sip of chocolate almond coffee. "You all right?" she asked me.

I glanced at my watch again. "When will Rose get here?"

Mama set her empty cup on a table. "You're a city girl, you're not ready to go to bed, are you?" she asked.

"No, I'm not ready to go to bed, but I am ready to talk to Cliff. I promised him I'd call and I wanted to do it *after* Rose's secret visit," I replied, sounding more than a little impatient.

Mama's eyebrow rose just as the phone rang. I picked it up. "Miss Candi?" the voice on the other end asked.

"No," I answered. "Who is this?"

"Rose."

"Just a minute." I handed the phone to Mama.

"Candi speaking," Mama said. "Okay," she said, then handed the receiver back to me to hang up.

"Is she still coming?" I asked.

"Yes, she's still coming. She'll be here in fifteen minutes. Simone, you might as well be prepared—Rose is tired, so she's asked Nightmare to drive her here."

"You've got to be kidding!" I exclaimed, irritated. Nightmare had been among Rose's guests, but he hadn't come anywhere near me, which suited me fine. I crossed my arms across my chest. "I should've known that I'd have to deal with that bad dream again."

"They won't stay long," Mama said.

Half an hour later, I opened Mama's door and stepped aside as Rose and Nightmare entered our foyer.

Rose, who now wore a long black dress that buttoned down the front from her neck to her ankles, and who held a brown paper bag tightly in her hands, walked in and smiled at me vaguely. Nightmare followed. His smirky gaze held mine for a few seconds.

"I'm sorry I'm so late," Rose told Mama.

Mama smiled graciously. "Sit down here by me," she said to Rose. Then she looked up at Nightmare. "Son, what is your name?" she asked.

He grinned. His straggly beard jounced up and down like it was being controlled by a puppet's string. "Call me Nightmare, Mr. James's wife," he answered.

I cleared my throat. "Sounds like the perfect name to me," I said.

Mama shot me a quick scolding look, then said, "I don't want to call you that name. What name did your mama give you when you was born?" she insisted.

Nightmare looked down at his hands, but he didn't say anything.

"His mama named him Dan, but he won't answer to it," Rose said.

"Nightmare is a good name 'cause I like to scare pretty women," he said, giving me a direct look, his eyes dark, disturbing. Refusing to be intimidated by him, I stared back, trying hard not to squirm. His look made my skin crawl.

Mama cleared her throat, then she fixed her gaze on Nightmare. "Sit down, Dan," she said, pointing to a chair.

Nightmare broke off eye contact with me. He

shoved his hands in his pockets and looked around the room, but he didn't move from his spot right in the doorway.

I perched on the arm of a black leather chair and waited. Actually, I was thinking that I should have gotten my can of Mace from the car.

Rose gestured in irritation. "Did you hear Miss Candi tell you to sit down?" she snipped at Nightmare.

He shifted uncomfortably on his feet. But he didn't move.

"Okay, Dan," Mama told him, her voice unperturbed. "Stand right there until it's time for you to go."

Nightmare shook his head emphatically but still he didn't move.

Mama turned to face Rose. "What did you want to show me?" she asked.

"Well, Miss Candi," Rose began, looking down at the brown paper bag in her hand. "I was dusting those old books of Grandma Lucy Bell's this morning. You know, getting ready for people to come to the house after the funeral and all—"

"Yes," Mama prodded.

Rose held out the wrinkled old bag. "I don't know if you wanted to see this, but—well, this is what dropped out of one of them."

Mama took the bag.

Rose continued, "It had a picture of Grandma Lucy Bell, the one I put on the mantel."

"A good picture," Mama said.

"And this list of names, and—this note," Rose finished uneasily.

Mama looked at the note and studied it. After a few moments, she read it out loud: *"Vengeance is mine."*

Rose touched Mama's arm. "You notice the note ain't written in the same handwriting as the list," she said. She paused. "I guess I can't get those notes Cricket found on her windshield out of my mind—I don't know if this note got anything to do with those notes or not."

Now Mama's expression changed. She became thoughtful. "Simone, get a pad and pencil," she ordered me.

I obeyed; I was used to taking relevant notes.

Once I had pad and pencil, Mama continued. "Now Rose, tell us again exactly what the three notes that were written to Cricket said."

"Best I can recollect," Rose replied, "the first one said, *Morgan is pretty enough to steal.* The second one said, *Tainted blood runs inside you.* And the third one was, *Morgan suppose to be mine.*"

"Is it possible," Mama asked, as if talking to herself, "that Morgan was stolen as a vendetta?"

Rose sat straight up in her chair. "A what?" she asked, looking confused.

"Revenge," I said. "Somebody trying to get even for something."

Rose gave me a quick, suspicious glance. "Revenge for what? Cricket nor Morgan never done anything to anybody that I know of."

"Maybe, but—" Mama began.

Rose cut in. "I think the so-called revenge has got something to do with crazy Timber killing Cricket and letting some woman steal Morgan from that baby's real family," she insisted.

"Maybe," I suggested, "it has something to do with Lucy Bell's cemetery."

Nightmare moved abruptly. His eyes narrowed, his nostrils flared. In a fierce voice he said, "Nobody better bother with Grandma Lucy Bell's babies—I take good care of them babies just like I'm suppose to do—I made a promise to her, on her dying bed."

"Now I know I should have gotten my Mace from the car," I said to myself.

Mama eyed me seriously.

I tried to flash a smile of apology but Mama continued to look unhappily at me.

Rose turned to Nightmare. "We all know that you do a good job of keeping that cemetery nice and clean," she told him.

As suddenly as his anger had blazed, Nightmare's calm returned. He leaned back against the wall, his mean dark eyes watching us, his face expressionless.

"Like I told you the other day, Miss Candi," Rose said, "I don't want what I've told you to be thrown all over Otis County—I don't cotton to people talking about my family's business."

Mama lifted her eyebrows politely. "And, just like I promised you the other day, you have our confidence. Doesn't she, Simone?"

I nodded. "You know me. I don't talk other people's business."

Mama's gaze stuck to mine but she didn't say a word.

"Then you don't think these papers mean anything?" Rose asked Mama.

"I didn't say that," Mama told her. "Let me think about this for a few days."

Rose stood up, smoothing her long dress with her hand. "We'd better get back to the house," she told Nightmare.

"May I keep this note? And this list?" Mama asked.

Rose stared at her. "Long as they don't fall into the wrong hands."

"They won't leave this house," Mama promised.

Rose motioned to Nightmare. "Like I told the rest of my people," she said as she headed for the door, "Timber can't expect no Christian burial 'cause he ain't bound for heaven, the way he took both Cricket and Morgan away from us."

Nightmare mumbled something that sounded like an agreement. Then he said, very clearly, "Timber better not bother with Grandma Lucy Bell's babies. I promised her I'd take care of them babies, and nobody better not mess with them."

CHAPTER

SEVENTEEN

The photographs I'd taken at the Childs cemetery lay spread neatly on Mama's kitchen table. I checked the birth and death dates on each tombstone against the names on the list that Rose had entrusted to Mama.

There were fourteen names on Miss Lucy Bell's list: Eyelet Combs, Tony Tabard, Ruby Ayer, Viola Anderson, Cora Bailey, Archie Bamberg, Billy Capers, Joe Ponds, Rick Ponds, Mickey Culler, Irene Folk, Julia James, Daniel Holland, and Pearl Johnson.

"Miss Lucy Bell must have delivered all fourteen babies although she buried only twelve in her private cemetery," I told Mama. "Except for two names, the names on Rose's list matches the names on all the tombstones."

"Which babies don't have a tombstone?" Mama asked.

"Joe and Rick Ponds," I answered.

Mama picked up the list and studied it.

I glanced at my watch.

"What time are you expecting Yasmine?" she asked, without looking up from the list.

"Any minute," I answered.

"Tell me again, Simone, why did you invite Yasmine to come down from Atlanta and spend the night with you?"

I smiled. I knew that Mama wanted me to spill my guts about what was going on in Yasmine's life. "She needs to get out of the city," I answered, trying to avoid the subject, even though I knew I couldn't.

Mama, who was still looking down at the list of names Rose had given her, lifted her head and stared at me. Her expression told me that she wasn't buying my story.

"Is that the only reason she's coming all the way from Atlanta just to turn around and go back tomorrow?" she asked.

"Yasmine and I need to talk," I told Mama.

Mama's eyes raised above her gold-rimmed eyeglasses. "Is there something wrong between you two?"

I shrugged. "Nothing that a little girl-talk won't straighten out," I said, matter-of-factly.

There was an awkward moment until the doorbell rang. "It's Yasmine," I said, gathering the photographs and tossing them in a drawer.

Mama got up as quickly as she could. "Give me a second to get to the couch," she said. The bell rang again.

"Just a minute!" I hollered toward the door as the bell sounded a third time.

Yasmine looked beautiful. Her makeup was perfect, her hair flawless. She wore a midcalf short-sleeved yellow cotton dashiki that softly draped her shapely body; it had swirling bold prints of brown, red, black, and green. She smelled sweet, and her easy smile made her look younger than her twenty-five years. The only flaw in her appearance was the thinly veiled uneasiness in her lovely eyes.

"You know," I said, "you're one beautiful *young* black woman."

Yasmine gave me a dead-eyed stare. I'd clearly said the wrong thing. "You look nice," I added hastily, realizing that my girlfriend had read something in what I'd just said that she didn't like. The misgiving in her eyes deepened, but this wasn't the time for me to try to explain or apologize. I reached for her overnight bag.

Yasmine picked up her own case. "I can carry my own bag," she said. "Just tell me where to drop it."

I pointed toward the end of the foyer. "Put your bag over there, I'll take it to your room later." She dropped her bag to the floor, then walked into the family room and greeted Mama. "Miss Candi, I'm sorry about your feet," she said.

Mama smiled warmly. "Yasmine, don't ever grow old," she teased. "First your eyes go, then your teeth, your feet, and before you know it, every part of your body has been overhauled. Getting old ain't for sissies."

Yasmine's grin looked like a grimace. "Getting old ain't what you're about, Miss Candi."

Mama pointed to the chair that Rose had sat in the night before. It stood close enough to the couch for her to reach out and touch whoever sat in it. "Sit down," she told Yasmine. "I get jealous when I see others standing on feet that aren't gift-wrapped like mine."

Surprisingly, Yasmine looked bewildered, like she didn't want to sit near Mama.

Mama waved her hand in the air. "Sit down, girl, and rest yourself."

Yasmine hesitated. She glanced at me in resignation, then she dropped heavily into the armchair. I dumped myself into my favorite seat, the leather chair near the sliding glass door.

Mama studied Yasmine. "You look like you don't feel good," she said. "Do you want something to eat, honey?"

Yasmine touched her hair, shook her head. "No, I'm not hungry."

But Mama ignored her. "Simone, get up and fix Yasmine a plate of that beef Stroganoff we had for supper."

"Girl," I told Yasmine, "Mama showed me her secret—the only thing that's missing is her hands blessing the ingredients."

Mama was pleased. "Simone followed my instructions, and the beef Stroganoff turned out pretty good."

Yasmine made a face. "No," she said, her voice choked. "I don't want anything to eat."

I flopped down in my chair, stunned. Yasmine's eyes looked teary. I realized that since we'd talked her problem had festered.

Mama nodded in acceptance rather than agreement. "Is it as hot in Atlanta as it is here?" she asked, her voice concerned.

Yasmine slumped in her chair. "I believe it's hotter in Atlanta than it is here," she answered, with even less control.

I didn't like the way my girlfriend was acting. Her body language flashed like a neon light. If she didn't get a grip, Mama would be all over her with questions. Mama had that look, like she'd picked up that something was a lot more serious than I'd led her to believe it was. I tried to give Yasmine a reassuring look.

But Yasmine stared beyond me, into the backyard, into Mama's garden. I tried to redirect her mood. "Girl, I know how hot Atlanta can be in the middle of the summer. One of the reasons I'm glad Mama and Daddy live within a few hours' drive is that it gives me a chance to get some cool country air."

"Yes," Yasmine said, as if she wasn't talking to me or Mama.

Mama shifted. She'd made a decision and I knew

what it was. She was going to find out exactly what Yasmine and I were trying to put over on her. "Is everything okay in Atlanta?" she asked Yasmine.

I was right. Mama was setting Yasmine up. She'd expected Yasmine to say no to the question she asked. But Yasmine was supposed to also complain about whatever it was that was wrong in Atlanta, and at the same time cover what was really on her mind, her own personal problem.

When Yasmine waited a while before answering, I released a relieved breath. She wasn't going to take Mama's bait. Then tears began to seep out of the corners of Yasmine's eyes, dropping down her pretty face. "Nothing has changed, nothing will ever change—"

"Everything changes," I cut in, my last-ditch effort to pull my friend through Mama's interrogation. "Life is continuous change," I added lightly, "don't you think so, Mama?"

Mama looked at me, then suddenly pulled herself up to her feet.

Yasmine glanced over at me, then wiped her wet cheeks with the back of her hand.

"I know that you and Simone want to be alone," Mama said. "I'll just go to my room."

"Miss Candi," Yasmine whispered, "you don't have to leave."

But Mama spoke quickly, as if she expected Yasmine to say that. "I want you to know that I respect your privacy, Yasmine. Besides, I've got a book I want to finish reading."

There was a brief silence, Mama giving us time to think. I cranked my neck to try to signal Yasmine not to say anything more so that Mama would go to her room, but now Mama stood between us, blocking my view.

Mama moved with such slow deliberation that there was a certain majesty in her motion. She passed Yasmine, walked toward the hall that led out of the family room into the foyer. She was in the doorway when Yasmine whispered softly, "Miss Candi, please don't go."

I stared at Yasmine, not knowing what to say.

Mama turned and looked as if she'd just come to some decision. Her expression hadn't changed except that maybe her eyes seemed wider at their corners. Her voice was quiet. "You want to talk to me and Simone together?" she asked Yasmine.

"I—I think so," my girlfriend whispered.

I rubbed my forehead and wondered what to do. Make an effort, I thought, to lighten up the situation. I decided to make a joke out of Mama's exodus. "There's no reason for you to go to your room just 'cause I've got company," I said.

Mama didn't find my remark funny. She frowned.

"I could really use something to drink," Yasmine said. Her tone suggested that she was trying to regain her composure.

I hopped up and headed for the kitchen. The thought occurred to me that it might be good that Mama had cleverly manipulated Yasmine into letting her be a part of our talk. I was struggling to make sense of Yasmine's situation, and I still didn't know what I was going to say to her. I just knew that I wanted to talk her into changing her mind.

Mama looked satisfied. She eased back on the couch, stretched out again, smoothed the long black skirt she wore. In a few seconds, her feet were propped back up on her stack of pillows.

"What about you, lady?" I asked Mama. "Would you like something to drink?"

Mama looked at Yasmine. Then she said, "Fix me and Yasmine a cup of that fresh-perked Irish cream coffee."

Yasmine fumbled in her purse, pulled out a handkerchief, and wiped her eyes.

"And," Mama continued, "cut us a piece of that red velvet cake you found in the freezer this morning, Simone." She flashed a smile that both Yasmine and I understood—Mama was very glad that she'd been invited to share our secret.

CHAPTER

EIGHTEEN

Yasmine's tears were gone now. A little voice in the back of my mind suggested that they had been deliberate. Maybe she *really* wanted Mama to be a part of this all along. Anyway, she barely touched her cake. Her hand gripped the handle of her coffee mug but she didn't touch that, either.

Mama sipped her coffee slowly, every now and again giving Yasmine a long look, one that said we were very willing to wait until Yasmine wanted to talk to us.

I took a sip of my coffee, put down the cup, and tasted my red velvet cake. It was soft, rich, like cotton candy melting in my mouth. I ate half, took a breath, and finished the rest.

My eyes rested on Yasmine's face. This warm,

witty, bright, fun-loving black woman looked utterly miserable. I couldn't believe that she was the girlfriend I'd go to whenever I wanted to have fun, whenever I needed to lighten up. "Yasmine," I said, "tell Mama what this is all about."

Yasmine put her cup down. "I don't want Miss Candi to think bad of me."

"I'm not going to judge you," Mama told Yasmine quietly, and I knew she meant it.

Yasmine thought for a moment before answering. "Miss Candi, I'm pregnant."

Mama didn't flinch. "I suspected you were," she said. "It's not an uncommon occurrence."

"I don't want to have a baby, so I've decided to terminate the pregnancy," Yasmine said.

I felt a shiver down my spine, but I knew better than to interrupt. Mama would be furious if I did that. Mama didn't make any movement; she didn't react at all. "Is that what you really want to do?" she asked.

Yasmine hesitated, long enough for me to begin to hope that she really was having second thoughts. "I've got to do it," she finally said, her voice low. She refused to make eye contact with either me or Mama, choosing instead to look out into the garden where twilight cast eerie shadows. The foyer clock chimed eight.

"As I understand it, Yasmine, you're pregnant and you're going to have an abortion?" Mama asked.

"That's right."

"It's not something you want to do, but it's something you *feel* you have to do?"

Yasmine started to answer, but decided not to. Instead, she nodded.

I couldn't hold back any longer. "She doesn't have to have an abortion," I said. "She won't be the only single parent—"

Yasmine cut in. "I don't want to be a single parent. I want a husband, a home—"

Mama leaned forward. "Being pregnant doesn't stop you from having those things," she told us.

"It does when the father of your baby doesn't know you're pregnant," I snapped. "When you make a decision to have an abortion without bothering to tell him."

"I'm not making Ernest marry me just because I'm pregnant!" Yasmine exclaimed angrily.

"Give him that right," I said, my voice rising. "Give him the chance to stay or walk away before you do something you'll regret the rest of your life."

"It's easy for you," Yasmine shouted at me. "You don't want a husband, you don't want babies."

"Who told you that?"

"I don't have to be a Philadelphia lawyer to know that your only interest in my pregnancy is to satisfy your own self-righteousness," my girlfriend shot back, her voice cold, harsh.

I was dumbfounded. "Girl," I said, "you're really tripping now. I want a husband, a house, children, and—"

"And I want grandchildren," Mama interrupted calmly, motioning me back into my seat. "But I don't have the right to make those demands on you, Simone, now do I?" she asked me.

"What do you mean?"

"You have no right to impose your feelings on Yasmine," Mama told me, her voice low, direct.

Yasmine's angry expression changed. "Simone, girl, I don't want you to *tell* me what to do. I just want you to go with me to the clinic to give me support."

Mama looked at Yasmine. "It's not right that you should ask Simone to do that," she told her.

Yasmine's mouth opened, but nothing came out. I guess Mama had surprised both of us, Yasmine and I.

"Listen, you two," Mama continued. "Yasmine, you've got the right to decide what to do with your body, and Simone doesn't have any recourse but to accept that decision."

Yasmine nodded.

"On the other hand," Mama added, "you've got to understand, Yasmine, that Simone has got the right to refuse to support you in doing something that she's against."

We both stared at Mama.

"The solution to this is acceptance, pure and simple," Mama concluded, leaning back in the sofa. "Accept how each other feels, and allow your friendship to go from there."

Yasmine looked at me, her eyes wide and still

angry. "How can you call a person your friend if she won't stick with you through thick and thin?"

"A friend is a person who will tell you things straight," Mama said with a little edge in her voice, like she was impatient with Yasmine and me for being so childlike. "A person who won't bend simply to satisfy your feelings. The fact that Simone is sticking to her guns on this, even though she knows it's hurting you, means that you can trust her, Yasmine. The next time an issue comes up that you need honest feedback on, you know Simone is the one friend who won't play games with you. She's a shooter from the hip, not one that aims behind your back."

I fiddled with one of the rings I wore, thinking that Mama was making me sound uncomfortably noble.

"On the other hand, Simone . . ." Mama continued to me. I suppose I should have known better than to think I'd get away with just a compliment. Mama tapped her temple with her index finger. "Simone, think," she said. "Suppose you wanted to do something that Yasmine was against. How would you feel if she tried to block you, tried to take away your right to make a decision that affects your life?"

I nodded; Mama was making me understand.

"The important thing is that Yasmine decides what she wants to do without imposing that decision on anybody else. Whatever the results, it's Yasmine who will bear it alone."

Yasmine shifted in her chair, her expression suddenly tinged with uncertainty. "Do *you* think I should tell Ernest about this baby?" she asked Mama.

"Yes!" I blurted.

Mama took a deep breath, then shook her head. "I don't think either of you heard a word I said."

"Yes, we did," I said. "And I agree with you, Mama. But I can't help but make at least one more effort to keep Yasmine from doing something that will hurt her."

Yasmine's face tightened.

"Yasmine, you accused me of not wanting a husband, children," I said. "The fact is that I do want those things."

Yasmine stared silently at me while I stopped and thought once more about what I was about to say. Mama watched me thoughtfully. I continued, "I know now that the truth is that I've been repressing my so-called maternal feelings because I was scared. Scared that I couldn't measure up to being as good of a mother as Mama has been to Will, Rodney, and me.

"Yasmine, I guess what I'm saying is that I do know how the thought of being a parent can be overwhelming—"

"I'm not scared of being a good mother," Yasmine interrupted. "I *know* I can bring this kid up right. It's just that—" She stopped and looked nervously between me and Mama. "Do you think I should tell Ernest that I'm pregnant?" she asked Mama again.

Mama smiled reassuringly. "It's your decision, honey. Yours alone."

Yasmine still looked doubtful. "If Ernest walks, I'm having an abortion."

"He won't walk," I told her. "I just know he'll want you. And your baby."

"Whether you go with me to the clinic or not, Simone, I'm not bringing this kid into the world without a husband."

Mama smiled and nodded. "It's not easy being a single parent, but it is possible to raise kids alone."

Yasmine's eyes hardened. "I don't want to raise my kid without a husband."

Mama looked as if Yasmine's decision was satisfactory. "It's your life," she said, in a tone that made me conscious of the important lesson I'd just come to understand about myself. Facing my fear of not being as good a mother as my mama was something that would change my life and my relationship with Cliff.

NINETEEN

The next afternoon, we breathed the sweetness of magnolia blossoms from the enormous tree that stood on the opposite side of the gravel driveway as we waved good-bye to Yasmine. It was close to three o'clock.

I was very drained and a little depressed. After Mama had left the room the night before, Yasmine and I talked for hours. We paced the room and spoke about the things that frightened us, the things that were important to us.

We talked about my father and I shared glimpses of memories I had of him, times when I was glad he was there for me, times when I felt his presence in quiet and wise ways.

Yasmine told me that her parents had never

married, that she'd only heard bad things about her dad from her mother's people. She recalled, with a deep chill in her voice, that she'd spent most of her life fantasizing about him. "Imagine having a relationship with an illusion," she said. She shook her head. "I don't want my child to feel that pain," she whispered.

Hours later, at dawn, it struck us that we had to do more than sit and talk about our feelings. Mama was right: we had to accept our fears; we had to move on.

"It's easier to say that I'll give Ernest up than to actually do it," Yasmine had said about her decision to give Ernest an ultimatum about her need for marriage, children, family.

Her words reminded me of what Mama had said to me time and again over the years. I repeated them just the way she'd said them. "No matter how hard it may be, there are times when we've got to go beyond our emotions and do what's right, for ourselves, for our children, for our families—"

Neither of us spoke after that. We fell asleep, and five hours later we jumped up, ate something, and kept talking until Yasmine had to drive back to Atlanta.

No sooner had Yasmine driven out of sight than a familiar blue sedan drove up into our driveway.

I groaned. The very sight of Nightmare made me uneasy. But Mama watched him without expression as he jumped out of his battered old car.

His face and powerful upper body glistened with sweat. His clothes were streaked with what I hoped was animal blood. The wind shifted; his odor was nauseating. I stiffened.

Just for a moment, Nightmare's eyes found mine and grabbed hold. I gave him a cold stare, determined not to show fear.

Nightmare grinned. He mopped his sweaty face and asked, "Mr. James home?"

Mama leaned back on the porch rail and flashed Nightmare an easy smile. "We expect James soon," she answered. "You want to come in and wait for him?"

I almost fainted. She couldn't seriously expect this man to sit in our house waiting for my father!

Nightmare's smile widened. Yellow, crooked teeth showed through his straggly beard. He shook his head. "Tell Mr. James that Nightmare just dropped off cleaned venison, rabbit, and squirrel at Mr. Coal's house—half be his and half be Mr. Coal's."

As Mama's mouth opened to thank him, Midnight came running from the backyard, barking wildly. The dog shot forward, leaping at Nightmare and then, standing on his hind legs, his body wriggling, he pawed and licked his face so hard that he pushed Nightmare back two unsteady steps. He nearly knocked the big man over.

Mama's brows went up. "Seems like Midnight knows you," she said.

As Midnight yapped, Nightmare grinned and rubbed the dog's ears. "Good dog," he told Midnight. To Mama, he said, "I was there the day this dog's mama dragged him from underneath old man

Ponds's back porch. He used to follow me around as a puppy."

Mama's eyes widened like something had suddenly worked across her mind. She cocked her head. "You mean the old man Buck Ponds that died about six months ago?" she asked.

Nightmare kept stroking Midnight with his right hand. He wiped his forehead with the sleeve of his left arm. "Yessmm," he answered.

Mama's brow wrinkled. "Didn't he live about two miles from here?"

"About that far," Nightmare responded.

Mama turned to me. Her eyes were bright. "Could it be that I was wrong," she mouthed, then stopped as a red ten-year-old Buick swung into our driveway. Carrie Smalls parked beside Nightmare's car. Still playing with Daddy's dog Midnight, Nightmare paid her no mind.

"More company," I grumbled under my breath. Oddly, Mama looked pleased.

But Nightmare's face had clouded. He nudged Midnight away, then strode toward his car.

Midnight glanced at the three women, then lumbered underneath the magnolia tree and flopped down on the grass, his muzzle tucked between his front paws. He kept his eyes expectantly on Nightmare.

Nightmare wasn't watching the big black dog. Instead, he watched these three women, an odd timidity now in his expression. I suspected that he, like Rose and maybe the rest of his family, harbored some deep emotion or fear of things they'd say about him. Anyway, he looked like he thought they got as much pleasure out of talking about everybody in the town as he enjoyed scaring women. "I reckon I'd better go," he said curtly, and swung open his car door. Midnight raised his head, watching.

"Wait a minute. Wait," Mama said. She had to raise her voice because Nightmare had turned on his engine. "I want to ask you a question before you leave."

Nightmare squinted his eyes. Then he nodded bleakly and switched off his car.

The three women struggled out of their car and approached us. Mama turned to face her new guests. She adjusted her glasses. "Ladies," she said, "it's real nice to see you."

"Candi," Sarah Jenkins gasped, like she was out of breath, "we just had to come tell you—"

A look of impatience flitted across Annie Mae Gregory's face as she cut in. "Rick Martin told us that they've picked up Timber."

Carrie Smalls's thin body was erect, her arms folded stoically across her breast. "Nabbed him in Rome right across the county line," she contributed. "Darn fool was trying to rob Double B Feed & Seed store."

I glanced at Mama, who still looked like the whiff of something she'd remembered nagged at her. "Simone, show these ladies inside the family room, give them a cold drink, a piece of that red velvet cake."

"You stood at a stove and baked a cake with your feet ailing?" Sarah Jenkins asked, looking down at Mama's bandaged feet. "When I had my feet worked on, I couldn't get near a stove for at least three or four weeks."

Mama's smile was more with her eyes than her mouth. "I baked it before I had the surgery, Sarah. It's one of those recipes that gets better after it's been stored in the freezer for a while."

Annie Mae's eyes, buried in fat, shone greedily. "I could use a cold drink and a piece of that cake about now," she admitted, with a laugh.

But Sarah Jenkins stared at Mama. "I tell you it's so hot today that a body could get a heatstroke. Really, Candi, I don't think it's good for you to be out. If I remember right, the doctor warned me not to be out in this. Course he knows about my various ailments, knows the many medications I have to take."

I shrugged. I wasn't in the mood to hear Sarah Jenkins expound on her ailments or her many medications. I waved the women past me and Mama, up the steps, and into the house.

But Mama didn't move to come inside. Instead, she looked thoughtfully at Nightmare. Once the women had entered into the foyer in front of me, out of hearing range, Mama spoke softly to Nightmare. "Dan, when was the last time that you was on the Pondses' place?"

I glanced back at Nightmare. His jaw muscles

flexed, he gave a kind of a groan, but he didn't say anything.

"Remember, Rose told us that he's too stubborn to answer to any name except Nightmare," I reminded Mama. I added, "It's a good name for him 'cause he's the closest thing to the boogeyman that I've ever seen."

Mama didn't say anything to either of us for a second or two. "Okay," she said, her voice low, exasperated. "*Nightmare*, when was the last time you were on the Pondses' place?"

CHAPTER

TWENTY

"I declare, Candi." Annie Mae Gregory's words were indistinct because her mouth was full. She was chewing on a piece of red velvet cake. "You should be paid good money for your baking." Her big jaws, her double chin, and her greedy mouth made me wonder how many times she'd made this comment to somebody else.

Mama, who had settled on the couch, waved dismissively. "I do a fair job."

I yawned, then sat in my favorite chair. It would be another two hours before Daddy would be home. I felt I needed at least half that time to recoup from Yasmine's visit, but I was pretty sure that wouldn't happen.

Carrie Smalls sat up straight, her neck like a crane, her narrow hands folded precisely in her lap. "I suppose they'll bring Timber back to Otis County, don't you think?" she asked Mama.

Sarah Jenkins coughed and suddenly all our eyes were on her. She smirked, like she was pleased at our attention, then cleared her throat. "I get that tickle every now and again. I told the doctor about it, but he didn't think to give me a prescription."

"What do you think, Candi?" Annie Mae Gregory asked, dabbing her mouth with a napkin. "You think, like Carrie, that Abe can get Sheriff Shaw of Rome to turn Warren and Timber over to him?"

Mama nodded. "Abe will have to question Timber," she answered absently. Mama shifted in her chair like she didn't want to talk about Cricket, Timber, or Warren. "Carrie," she asked, finally getting to what was really on her mind, "you know much about Buck Ponds?"

Miss Carrie glanced at each of her companions before answering Mama's question. "I know as much as to be known about the old coot," she admitted.

Mama took a deep breath, leaned back, then crossed her arms in front of her, as if she was preparing her mind to take a journey. "Good," she said, clearly satisfied.

A glint of surprise flashed in Carrie Smalls's dark eyes; a deep scowl formed between her eyebrows. I would have sworn that she wanted to know why Mama had asked about Buck Ponds. This was not the way I expected her to look. After all, never before had these women needed understanding to recount details of their neighbors' lives.

"Tell me about Buck," Mama said.

Carrie Smalls replied, "His mind was bad, he did crazy things—"

Sarah cut in. "Nobody had much to do with him after they found out what he did."

Carrie turned to Sarah. "That's 'cause what he did wasn't *natural*."

Annie Mae Gregory, whose eyes had large dark circles around them like a raccoon's, added, "Especially to his own."

Sarah Jenkins leaned forward. "When Buck's wife, Rebecca, died twenty years ago, this county saw the biggest funeral it'd ever seen."

Carrie nodded. "That's a fact."

Sarah seemed pleased. "Folks came from all over—Course, I always thought Rebecca was a little on the silly side."

Annie Mae Gregory spoke. "I expect the news from the church board was what killed her."

Carrie's thin neck stretched further. "I'd have killed *him* 'fore it killed me," she said firmly.

Mama listened quietly. I groaned to myself. It took forever to pull a coherent story out of these three. I blurted out, "Did Buck Ponds *kill* his wife?"

Sarah Jenkins looked over at me, surprised by my question. "Buck might as well have taken a knife and plunged it into Rebecca's heart."

"When she found out what he done, it killed her," Carrie said.

Annie Mae Gregory nodded. "Most folks agreed with you."

Mama frowned. "What did Buck Ponds do that was so bad that it caused his wife to die?"

Sarah Jenkins's thin body twitched like she'd felt a chill. "It's too contemptible to tell."

I couldn't help wondering what anybody could have done that was too contemptible for these women to gossip about. But for once I was too smart to make a sarcastic comment. I sat down and tried to be patient.

Mama leaned forward. "I'd like to know," she prompted.

Carrie Smalls's face hardened. "When Buck Ponds died, not more than five people showed up at the church. And I was told not one of them went with his body to the cemetery."

"Serves him right," Sarah added. " 'Cause of what he'd done, they wouldn't let those poor little things be buried in the church's graveyard."

I stood up, exasperated, but Mama's eyes flashed toward me. I got her message: I sat back down.

Mama smiled, a different smile from the one she'd had earlier. Her meaning was clear. She was going to sift through the tidbits of information these women were giving one crumb at a time until she got what she wanted. "I suppose I should remember Buck and Rebecca," she mused, "but I can't for the life of me place them."

Sarah Jenkins shook her head. "Rebecca died

while you was all over the world running after the government and that husband of yours."

"Daddy was in the Air Force," I had to say.

Sarah ignored me. "Buck lived on his place like a hermit until he died a little over six months ago."

I'd had it. "Tell us what happened and stop beating around the bush," I pleaded.

Mama eyed me again, but this time she didn't say anything.

Sarah looked at me as if she didn't care that this dialogue was getting on my nerves, then she turned to Mama. "Mind you, Candi," she said, lowering her voice. "I ain't saying Buck was the *only* one responsible for what he did."

I was amazed at Mama's patience. But I sensed this story was so important for her to hear that she was willing to let these women tell it in their own way.

I turned to look out into the garden, to watch the sunlight slant through the oak tree. There wasn't anything for me to do but to wait. Mama seemed determined to get what she wanted without pushing.

Annie Mae Gregory spoke. "That gal was ten, but she should have told Rebecca what her daddy was doing to her."

"So, the Pondses had a child, a daughter?" Mama asked.

The three women nodded. Sarah Jenkins belched. "The Lord is good," she declared. " 'Cause that girl turned out better than anybody would have thought she would."

"Especially since things like that spread through the town and people have such long memories," Annie Mae Gregory added.

Mama's eyes sparkled.

Annie Mae Gregory sighed deeply. "About twenty-two years ago, Buck Ponds had unnatural relations with his only child, his daughter. I suspect 'cause she was so young and her body wasn't fully formed, it was natural that she would give birth to sickly twin boys."

"What happened to the two babies?"

"Those two twin babies died four months after they were born," Sarah said candidly, like she was proud of knowing the fact.

"Who was the midwife who waited on the Ponds girl?" Mama asked.

"Lucy Bell Childs," Carrie Smalls said.

Mama's eyes shone brighter than the morning star. She breathed deeply as if now she understood all.

Annie Mae Gregory spoke. "Somehow or another, Rebecca Ponds found out that Buck had got the girl pregnant. The poor woman got sick when her grand-babies came; she was doing even more poorly when they died. When the preacher and the other church members wouldn't let those two poor babies be buried in the church cemetery 'cause of how they were conceived, it was too much for Rebecca to bear. She died three days later. Her sister, Cassie Tuten, who lives on the county line between Rome and Otis, came and took the girl to finish raising her."

"Where were the twins finally buried?" Mama asked.

"I declare, Candi, I don't rightly know. Nobody had anything else to do with Buck."

"It would be against the law to bury the children on his own property," I said.

"Simone," Mama said, "in Otis, the burial laws aren't as strict or as enforced as they are in a big city like Atlanta." She addressed the women again. "Did this girl have any more children?"

Annie Mae Gregory shook her head. "Naw, but she got married."

Carrie Smalls added, "She's done pretty good for herself, don't you think?" she asked her two companions.

When they nodded, I could see that Mama was satisfied, she'd learned all she needed. "I suspect that girl, who is now a woman, lives here in Otis, doesn't she?" Mama asked.

"Lord, yeah," Carrie Smalls exclaimed. "She's been living here ever since the first day Isaiah Smiley married her!"

THREE

Nightmare snapped his fingers and made a gesture. Instantly, Midnight understood his command. The dog scrambled to his feet, wriggled happily when the big man's huge hand patted his sleek head, then they started to walk.

This time there was no stopping to sniff a tree trunk, a clump of ivy, a fallen limb. This time the dog trotted obediently alongside his companion.

The narrow, winding path seemed longer today. Midnight hesitated as they passed the maple, the oak whose limbs met overhead, making a shadowy tunnel that let only a dappling of sunlight break through.

An experienced hunter, Nightmare was careful to stay away from roots or rocks that might cause a twisted ankle. Nightmare spoke, and although the dog couldn't understand the big man's words, he knew that he was doing what Nightmare wanted him to do. Midnight made a soft sound and wagged his tail.

A breeze stirred the leaves overhead. A patch of rolling leaves sent an interesting scent the dog's way; Midnight hesitated. "Go on," Nightmare's deep voice encouraged. But this time Midnight didn't obey. Instead, he sniffed at the pile of leaves, turned in a circle, and squatted. Nightmare seemed satisfied to wait.

Once he'd finished, Midnight walked along the path, sniffing the air. He smelled fire and the scents of something cooking. He stopped. The dog felt confused, especially when his ears were shocked by an unfamiliar sound.

He looked up at Nightmare, who now turned and looked back. Midnight wasn't surprised. He had smelled his master and the two white men who were following them.

Ahead of them was the old shack. Midnight's ears pricked; he picked up a sound that interested him.

Midnight knew that the crying baby inside the shack posed no threat to him, so he decided to dash ahead, push past the house to what was most important. When he stopped again, he wasn't far from the back door. He put his nose to the ground, and turned in a complete circle. Then, like before, he began digging.

CHAPTER

TWENTY-ONE

We had a whole lot of reasons to be thankful this Thanksgiving weekend. Mama's feet were better; she had returned to work. And to her kitchen.

But there was another very special reason. If you'd looked at Yasmine, you'd see that she waved graceful hands, tinted nails glossed to perfection. On both her and Ernest's ring fingers were matching wedding bands.

Yasmine had told Ernest he had the option of marriage and the baby or she'd abort. The next morning Ernest woke her early and carted her off to City Hall to get a license. Three days later, Cliff and I joined them as they were married in a civil ceremony.

Mama's table was set. The delightful aroma of the

twenty-five-pound roasted turkey stuffed with a
corn-bread-and-pecan dressing wafted from the center of the table. There were also cranberry sauce, candied sweet potatoes, macaroni and cheese, collard
greens, white rice, field peas and okra, string beans
and white potatoes, carrot soufflé, and homemade
yeast rolls. My mouth watered at the sight of it.
Mama had used her best china, her silverware and
crystal. Her guests: Cliff and I, Ernest and Yasmine,
my brothers Rodney and Will and, of course, my
father.

It was Ernest who turned the conversation to
the kidnapping of Cricket's baby. "Miss Candi," he
said, "I heard you cleaned up another one of Otis's
scandals."

Mama looked like she was thinking back as she
surveyed our questioning eyes without answering
Ernest. Daddy's fork swung in midair. "If it wasn't
for Candi," he bragged, "Lord only knows what that
crazy woman would have done to that poor baby."

"James, I don't think Birdie would have harmed
little Morgan," Mama murmured.

Daddy looked at Mama like she was being too
modest. "She's on Bull Street in Columbia. Like I
said, ain't no telling what she'd have done to that
poor kid if you hadn't told Abe where to find them."

I leaned over and whispered to Cliff: "Bull Street
is the state hospital for crazy people."

Cliff nodded.

"Tell us about how she stole that baby and why

she did it," Ernest urged Mama. "Start from the beginning."

Mama leaned back and surveyed her waiting audience. Then she said, "When Birdie was ten years old, her father got her pregnant," she began. "The poor child delivered a set of twin boys. But those babies died when they were only four months old."

"Tell them how Lucy Bell Childs got involved," I prompted.

Mama's eyes flashed at me, but she continued. "During the time, Lucy Bell Childs was the prominent midwife here in the county. It seemed that all of her babies contracted some fever which caused them to linger sickly until they died, about six months after their birth. The talk got around that Lucy Bell carried the fever, so she ended up with the sickly babies, nursing them until they died. She buried them in the little cemetery in the back of Rose's mobile home.

"Like I told Simone earlier, the burial laws ain't as strict in these parts as in a big city, and the laws that we do have ain't fiercely enforced. Once you're out in the country, past the town limits, things get so slack people can do most anything they want to as long as nobody complains. So, since nobody complained, Lucy Bell decided to bury those babies in the little cemetery in the back of Rose's mobile home."

"I didn't even know there was a cemetery behind those trailers," Daddy volunteered.

"I didn't either, James," Mama said. "But, from the first time I noticed when Simone and I visited

Rose to pay our respects over Cricket's death, I was intrigued. It was like something drew me to the little graveyard, something made me think that it was tied to Morgan's disappearance."

I nodded. "That's why she had me crawling around on my hands and knees taking pictures of the tombstones."

Mama smiled. "Back to Birdie and Lucy Bell Childs," she said, returning to her story. "Even though Lucy Bell no longer worked at delivering babies, Birdie's mother, Rebecca Ponds, called on her to help Birdie during her labor."

"For heaven's sake, why?" Yasmine exclaimed.

"Yasmine, honey, I don't rightly know," Mama answered. "I can only guess that it was because Rebecca was too ashamed to call in another midwife or even to take Birdie to a doctor or a hospital."

Nobody spoke, thinking of poor Rebecca's shame and misery, all those many years ago.

"But it's important to note that Lucy Bell didn't take care of these twins like she'd taken care of the other babies she delivered, the ones who'd caught the fever.

"Lucy Bell Childs must have grown to love the twelve babies she took care of, because she made her grandson, Dan, vow to take care of the cemetery."

"Nightmare must have been about fifteen at the time," I said, chewing a piece of sweet potato.

"How did you figure that Birdie had stolen the baby, Mama?" my brother Will asked.

Mama looked across the table at her son. "When

Rose brought me the note that she'd found in one of Lucy Bell's old books, a list of names was with it. Simone and I compared the names on the list to the ones on the tombstones."

"I took pictures of each grave," I said.

"The names of the Ponds twins were on the list, but those two babies didn't have headstones in the cemetery," Mama continued. "I figured maybe they weren't buried there. Midnight brought home two skulls. I was sure he hadn't gotten them from that graveyard—there was no sign of digging. When Dan, Rose's cousin—"

"Nightmare," I interrupted.

Mama raised her eyebrows and said, "When Dan told me that Midnight had been born on the Pondses' place, coupled with the fact that Midnight first showed up at our house about the time old Buck Ponds died, I surmised that dog might have gone back from time to time. So I asked Dan, who admitted that he frequented the Pondses' place to hunt. He confirmed my suspicion that Midnight had been digging in the old man's backyard.

"The day that we went to Cricket's funeral, I saw a station wagon with Birdie in it. It was a terrible rainstorm, it didn't make any sense for Birdie to be just sitting in her car outside of the church. Even more puzzling to me was that I saw Birdie in the station wagon on the road again when we were driving to Rose's house. I couldn't help but wonder whether I was wrong in thinking that she was back off her medication and that she wasn't functioning right."

"Why did Birdie kidnap Morgan?" Yasmine asked.

"Birdie's childhood was terribly traumatic. Her father, Buck Ponds, was an awful man. The doctor told Abe that when Birdie's mind first fixed on little Morgan Childs, it was simply because she thought Morgan was pretty. But when she stopped taking her medicine, she decided that Cricket wasn't a good mother because of her reputation. It wasn't too far a step for Birdie to begin thinking that Morgan should belong to her. Birdie believed that it was Morgan's great-grandmother, Miss Lucy Bell, who was responsible for the death of her own twin boys because the old midwife exposed her twins to the fever that killed them."

Yasmine still seemed puzzled. "But how did Birdie get Morgan?" she asked.

"Timber already believed that Cricket wasn't a good mother to his baby because of her association with Sabrina Miley, who was running a blackmail business on her gentlemen friends. It was easy for Birdie to give Timber money to buy liquor and at the same time encourage him to steal the child for her to care for. Timber told Cricket he was taking the baby to his mother for a few hours. Instead, he took Morgan and gave her to Birdie."

"Okay," I said, leaning back in my chair. "So Timber stole Morgan. But why did he kill Cricket?"

"Timber told Abe that news got to him that Clarence Young was working out of town for a few days. He decided it would be easy to break into

Clarence's empty apartment, to help himself to a few things. But Cricket found Timber in front of the Cherry Ridge Apartments a few seconds after he'd sprung Clarence's lock. Cricket started talking loud, demanding to know where Morgan was, who Timber had left Morgan with, yelling at Timber. Timber didn't want to draw attention to himself, so he took Cricket into Clarence Young's apartment. When Timber told Cricket that he'd given Morgan to a nice lady to be taken care of, Cricket went ballistic. According to Timber, he had to kill Cricket to keep her from killing him."

My brother Rodney waved his fork. "Is there enough evidence to convict Timber of killing Cricket?"

Mama nodded, her eyes sad. "Cricket's fingernails were torn and bloody. Scrapings from her nails held evidence of the skin of the person who killed her. The samples match Timber's DNA. And there were numerous bloodstains in the apartment where Cricket died. Some of those stains matched Timber's blood type, and samples of his hair were found on Cricket's body, her clothes. Timber's fingerprints were on a glass found inside the room. Cricket fought hard to stay alive. Yes, I think there will be plenty of forensic evidence to convict Timber when the case goes to trial."

There was a moment of silence.

"I have one last question," I said. "Why in the world did Birdie bring Morgan into the crowded Winn Dixie the first time she snatched her?"

Mama shook her head absently. "Poor Birdie was confused. It was one of those times when she didn't take her medicine. Like I said, without it, she can't think straight."

"Timber will probably get six or seven years, am I right?" Rodney asked Cliff.

Cliff nodded. "If an attorney can prove that it wasn't Timber's intent to murder Cricket, yes."

"Rose Childs's family was glad to have Morgan back with them. That poor child will have a good home for the first time in her life. I don't know when Birdie will be released from the hospital, but Isaiah told me that when she comes home, he'll personally make sure she'll keep taking her medicine."

"That sounds like a promise Isaiah Smiley has made before," I said.

Daddy pushed back in his chair. He reached across the table and touched Mama's hand. "Baby," he said, smiling, "you've outdone yourself with this meal. You've really outdone yourself this time."

And Mama smiled.

ABOUT THE AUTHOR

NORA DELOACH is an Orlando, Florida, native presently living in Decatur, Georgia. She is married and the mother of three. Her most recent Mama mystery is MAMA ROCKS THE EMPTY CRADLE, which is the fourth in the series, and she is currently at work on the fifth Mama mystery, MAMA PURSUES MURDEROUS SHADOWS.

Agatha Award–Nominated

TERI HOLBROOK

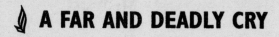

🔥 A FAR AND DEADLY CRY

Gale Grayson, expatriate American in England,
is drawn into the investigation of her
baby-sitter's brutal murder.

___56859-0 $5.99/$7.99 Canada

🔥 THE GRASS WIDOW

Upon her return home to Statlers Cross, Georgia,
Gale Grayson finds eccentric relatives and
a scandalous murder.

___56860-4 $5.50/$7.50 Canada

And now available in paperback

🔥 SAD WATER

___57718-2 $5.99/$8.99 Canada

Ask for these books at your local bookstore or use this page to order.

Please send me the books I have checked above. I am enclosing $____ (add $2.50 to
cover postage and handling). Send check or money order, no cash or C.O.D.'s please.

Name _____

Address _____

City/State/Zip _____

Send order to: Bantam Books, Dept.MC 29, 2451 S. Wolf Rd., Des Plaines, IL 60018
Allow four to six weeks for delivery.

Prices and availability subject to change without notice.   MC 29 1/99

GRACE F. EDWARDS

THE MALI ANDERSON MYSTERIES

"Excellent . . . Edwards expertly creates characters who leap to instant, long-remembered life."

—*CHICAGO TRIBUNE BOOK REVIEW*

"This girlfriend really cooks!"

—*MYSTERY LOVERS BOOKSHOP NEWS*

If I Should Die

___57631-3 $5.99/$7.99 IN CANADA

A Toast Before Dying

___57953-3 $5.99/$8.99 IN CANADA

HARLEM HAS NEVER BEEN HOTTER!

Ask for this book at your local bookstore or use this page to order.

Please send me the book I have checked above. I am enclosing $____ (add $2.50 to cover postage and handling). Send check or money order, no cash or C.O.D.'s please.

Name _____

Address _____

City/State/Zip _____

Send order to: Bantam Books, Dept. MC 23 , 2451 S. Wolf Rd., Des Plaines, IL 60018
Allow four to six weeks for delivery.
Prices and availability subject to change without notice.   MC 23 1/99

-DIANNE DAY-

Brave, resourceful, adventurous Fremont Jones is a woman ahead of her time...She's an investigator as perspicacious as Sherlock Holmes and as spirited as Kinsey Millhone.

THE STRANGE FILES OF FREMONT JONES

_____ 56921-X $5.99/$7.99 in Canada

FIRE AND FOG

_____ 56922-8 $5.99/$7.99 in Canada

THE BOHEMIAN MURDERS

_____ 57412-4 $5.99/$8.99 in Canada

EMPEROR NORTON'S GHOST

_____ 58078-7 $5.99/$8.99 in Canada

Ask for this book at your local bookstore or use this page to order.

Please send me the book I have checked above. I am enclosing $_____ (add $2.50 to cover postage and handling). Send check or money order, no cash or C.O.D.'s, please.

Name _____

Address _____

City/State/Zip _____

Send order to: Bantam Books, Dept. MC18, 2451 S. Wolf Rd., Des Plaines, IL 60018
Allow four to six weeks for delivery.
Prices and availability subject to change without notice.   MC 18 2/99